SO-AZY-987

> ## "Let me look, Grace. It's nothing I haven't seen before."

"No!" Grace's brows furrowed as she groaned. "Trust me. You haven't seen this." She pulled the bedsheets to her chin.

"Either you let me look, or I call a doctor." Brant was adamant.

"For pity's sake." She raised her caftan just enough for him to see her stomach.

He stared at her for a moment. "Lucky for you it's only a small watermelon."

"Brant!"

Brant knelt and leaned close, seeing a ridge appear in her belly. "What is that?"

Tentatively he reached out with a forefinger to touch her. Electricity shot through him as he felt the firmness of Grace's naked body. He touched the ridge, and it went away like magic. The wonder of it made Brant spread his entire palm over the place where the ridge had been. "Where did he go?" he whispered hoarsely.

"Maybe he was comforted by the feel of your hand and he's going back to sleep."

There was only one thing Brant could say through the thick cotton of his emotions. "Grace Barclay, I'm going to have to marry you."

Dear Reader,

His idea of a "long night" involves a sexy woman and a warm bed—not a squalling infant! To him, a "bottle" means champagne—not formula! Yeah, Brant Durning is about to get a big surprise. He's about to become an ACCIDENTAL DAD!

Tina Leonard takes you on a rollicking ride into parenthood—as macho cowboy and sworn bachelor Brant gets snagged by his sweetheart, Grace...and their bouncing bundle of joy!

The author of numerous romances, Tina Leonard makes her Harlequin debut. We're pleased to welcome her to Harlequin American Romance. Tina knows of what she writes—along with her family she makes her home in Texas and knows a good cowboy when she sees one!

Happy reading!

Debra Matteucci
Senior Editor & Editorial Coordinator
Harlequin Books
300 East 42nd Street
New York, NY 10017

COWBOY COOTCHIE-COO

TINA LEONARD

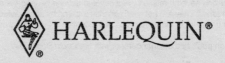

HARLEQUIN®

TORONTO • NEW YORK • LONDON
AMSTERDAM • PARIS • SYDNEY • HAMBURG
STOCKHOLM • ATHENS • TOKYO • MILAN • MADRID
PRAGUE • WARSAW • BUDAPEST • AUCKLAND

If you purchased this book without a cover you should be aware
that this book is stolen property. It was reported as "unsold and
destroyed" to the publisher, and neither the author nor the
publisher has received any payment for this "stripped book."

To my mother, Sylvia Avera Kalberer,
because she loved the Yellowjacket Cafe,
and
To Lisa, 8, and Dean Michael, 4, both growing up on me
too fast—thank you for believing in my dream,
And to my husband, Tim, for letting my dream be his.

ISBN 0-373-16748-2

COWBOY COOTCHIE-COO

Copyright © 1998 by Tina Leonard.

All rights reserved. Except for use in any review, the reproduction or
utilization of this work in whole or in part in any form by any electronic,
mechanical or other means, now known or hereafter invented, including
xerography, photocopying and recording, or in any information storage
or retrieval system, is forbidden without the written permission of the
publisher, Harlequin Enterprises Limited, 225 Duncan Mill Road,
Don Mills, Ontario, Canada M3B 3K9.

All characters in this book have no existence outside the imagination of
the author and have no relation whatsoever to anyone bearing the same
name or names. They are not even distantly inspired by any individual
known or unknown to the author, and all incidents are pure invention.

This edition published by arrangement with Harlequin Books S.A.

® and TM are trademarks of the publisher. Trademarks indicated with
® are registered in the United States Patent and Trademark Office, the
Canadian Trade Marks Office and in other countries.

Printed in U.S.A.

Chapter One

It ain't over till it's over. —Yogi Berra

Every eye in the Yellowjacket Cafe was on him. Brant Durning could feel the stares. His absence from Fairhaven, Texas, for the past three months hadn't gone unnoticed by the local residents—nor his return. He knew the topic of the day far outweighed interest in the soup of the day: What is Brant going to do about his wild little sister, Camille?

Sipping some iced tea, Brant supposed he'd given everyone plenty to be curious about. He caught Maggie Mason, the cook, watching him from her place behind the short-order line and grimaced. The grin on her face was telling. Before he had walked in to order lunch, no doubt the conversation had been centered on the fit he'd pitched when he returned to his ranch to discover the cows weren't the only things expecting offspring.

Cami had found a way to keep herself occupied with a man from a neighboring horse farm. Brant's brows furrowed. Shocked, and hurt for Cami's sake that there was no engagement ring on her finger, Brant had stormed her lover's house, demanding the man marry her at once and give a name to the child she carried.

Closing his eyes, Brant thought the only thing he'd left out of his outraged brother routine was a shotgun. He hadn't needed it. Cami's man had turned out to be more than eager to marry her, and the wedding plans were already in full swing—two weeks until the big day and counting.

"It ain't so bad, is it?"

Brant opened his eyes to see Maggie gazing at him as she slid into the cracked turquoise vinyl booth seat across from him. Her broad, ebony face was lit with impish laughter.

"Don't guess it's ever as bad as it seems," Brant replied. Maggie had known him all his life, even before he'd been old enough to drive himself to the Yellowjacket for mashed potatoes and greens. There wasn't any use in trying to act as if he didn't know what she was referring to.

"Nope, it's not." Her voice was amused. "Things were bound to change while you were away, Brant. Even in a small town, people's lives go on."

"Yeah." Of course, the interest-catching change had been in the Durning family. Why couldn't Cami have been more careful of her situation? Twenty-six was old enough to be able to stay out of trouble. As much as he loved Cami, her predicament was embarrassing.

"Everyone's going to think my cooking isn't agreeing with you. Your chin is hitting the table," Maggie told him.

He sighed and ran a hand absently across the back of his neck. "I'm all right, Maggie. I've got an errand to run that I'm not much looking forward to."

That was more truthful than he'd meant to be. Surprised by his own statement, Brant shifted his gaze to the plate-glass window. Across the street sat the next stop on his chore list. Wedding Wonderland was printed in big, scrolling white letters across the shop window. Customers walked into the two-story white building, itself almost resembling a wedding cake, coming out later carrying packages and wearing big smiles on their faces.

Once, going into the Wedding Wonderland had made him smile, too. Grace Barclay was the owner of the shop—and the only woman he'd ever come close to letting touch his heart. Today, he was going into her shop to pick up Cami's wedding gown, and there was nothing to make him smile about that.

Facing Grace after all these months made his stomach turn uncomfortably. Suddenly, Brant realized Maggie's delicious chicken-fried steak wasn't sitting too well with him. "I need to be getting on," he said.

Maggie nodded. "Tilly, bring Brant his check, please."

The tall, long-legged waitress laid a piece of paper at his elbow. Normally he enjoyed talking to the friendly waitress. Tilly was like everybody's little sister. Now all he could manage was a thin smile of thanks as he put enough money on the table to cover tab and tip.

"Thanks. Bye, Maggie." He got up, feeling the weight of the world on his shoulders. Nodding to a couple of regulars playing checkers at their customary table by the door, he hoped that would pass for a social amenity.

"Going somewhere?" Buzz Jones asked.

"Yep." Brant told himself Buzz's grin had always been that big, whether he had teeth or not.

"Heard tell there's going to be a wedding at the Double D," Purvis Brown called out.

There was no laughter at Brant's expense. It felt more like every ear in the cafe stretched out ele-phantlike to hear his reply. He settled his Stetson lower over his eyes. "You'll get your invitation, Purvis. Don't worry."

"Going to be a big hoedown, is it?"

"Big enough, I reckon. See ya." Brant left, unable to take the friendly ribbing a moment longer. Darn Cami for her recklessness! Standing outside on the cement walk, Brant stared unhappily at the Wedding Wonderland. Truth was, if he hadn't been so hot-headed with his visit to Cami's fiancé and family, no one in the town would have had much to talk about.

Unfortunately the situation was of his own mak-ing. Now, folks would be watching from behind the Yellowjacket's plate-glass window as he walked into the Wedding Wonderland empty-handed.

And they'd be watching when he came out car-rying a wedding gown.

He didn't want to do this. No three-month cattle buying trip, no keeping busy with the herds in the three months prior, had been able to wipe Grace out of his memory. She had always been there, in the smoky bars and the sensual laughter of other women. He'd told himself that the flame of their relationship had dwindled to a spark that couldn't burn his heart.

He had been lying to himself for six months.

I'm a fool to let Cami talk me into this. Cami, too ill with morning sickness that seemed to stretch all day, had pleaded with him to go pay the final installment on her wedding gown and bring it home. With the dimpled smile Brant had never been able to refuse, Cami claimed she might feel better if she could see her dream dress hanging in her own room.

Pushing the curved handle of the shop door, Brant wished he had never agreed to cross the threshold of the Wedding Wonderland. He cleared his throat, uncomfortable with the white decor and full-length mirrors around the room. The sensation of being out of his element was overwhelming.

"Just a minute. I'll be right with you," a woman called.

Brant's gut clenched at the sound of Grace's voice. She poked her head out from behind what appeared to be a fitting room door. Her mouth fell open. His glance skittered away before returning to brave her astonishment.

"Uh, hello, Brant."

All he could do was nod. Lord, how could she sound so casual? The tops of his ears felt as if they were on fire. Since Grace hadn't come out, all he could see was her face. When they'd been in love, he had thought she was the most beautiful woman he'd ever seen. Somehow, she was even more beautiful now.

"Is there something I can do for you?"

Again, he nodded. "I need to pick up Cami's wedding gown."

"Oh. I see." She seemed to think about that for a minute. "Um, I'm kind of busy right now. The gown is hanging on a rolling rack down that hallway if you don't mind getting it yourself."

Once upon a time, he would have done anything to wipe the strained expression from Grace's face.

Her blond hair was longer now, making her appear more feminine than ever. Her eyes were still huge and hazel and guaranteed to strike a man in his weakest moments. Brant told himself he wasn't having a weak moment right now.

"Fine. I'll do that." Though he wondered momentarily why she was sending him off in pursuit of his own purchase, he could only assume the woman wanted to avoid time in his company. The feeling was mutual, he told himself grumpily, as he searched through the stock tags on the gowns bearing customer names. He read each one a second time, but there was no gown tagged Durning. Glancing around to see if he might have missed another rolling rack, Brant decided Grace was just going to have to help him out on this one—no matter how awkward the situation.

He walked back out into the main salon. "I can't find it," he said. Her position was still defensive as she hovered behind the door. His remark didn't seem to make her happy, either.

"You couldn't find it? I was sure I hung it out."

He shrugged. She appeared to lose a shade of color in her face, which only made the pinpoint freckles he used to love to stroke with his finger stand out all the more.

"Could I have it sent around to your house this afternoon? I'm kind of tied up right now, and—"

"Cami really wanted to see her gown," Brant interrupted. He hesitated for a moment. "Grace, this isn't easy for either one of us. Actually it's worse than I thought it would be. But we have to live in the same town, run across each other once in a while.

Help me out here, Grace. I can't go home without that gown.''

"All right." She released an unhappy sigh, shooting him a wary look that nearly undid him. Those eyes of hers had always been his weakness. Slowly she stepped out from behind the door, holding a woman's undergarment in front of her.

But that didn't disguise what she'd obviously been trying to hide. Brant's jaw dropped.

"Grace—"

"This is a bustier." She pressed the undergarment to her midsection as she swished past him. "Some dresses require them. Cami won't need one with her—"

He caught her arm, turning her toward him, halting her un-Grace-like chatter. Slowly his gaze traveled over her body, cataloging extreme changes. "You're pregnant."

Her blush was painful to see.

"You came in to pick up your sister's gown, Brant," she said, meeting his stare. Pointedly she pulled her arm from his grasp. "If you'll excuse me, I'll go get it for you."

Brant couldn't believe his eyes as he watched Grace walk away from him. From the back, her figure had hardly changed. From the front, it was obvious she was in the advanced stages of pregnancy. He swallowed, jealousy pouring through him in a rush he never thought he'd feel. He'd protected his emotions far too long to feel this way. It shouldn't matter that Grace was having another man's baby.

She came back, carrying a profusion of shiny satin and frothy lace under clear protective wrappings. "Would you believe it was still in the stockroom?

My seamstress just finished making the alterations this morning. I hope Cami will be pleased.'' She thrust the gown into Brant's arms. ''Please tell your sister to let me know if there's anything else I can do for her.''

''You can do something for me.'' Brant didn't want to know the answer. All the same, he had to find out. ''You can tell me how long it took after we broke up for you to find someone else.''

He felt as if he was dying. Sure, they'd broken up, but that didn't mean he had ever stopped thinking about her. Every morning as he shaved, every night as he tried to fall asleep, he thought about the woman he just couldn't marry.

Apparently she hadn't been missing him too much. She looked angry. ''That's none of your business.''

He wanted to know who she was sleeping with. There was no ring on her finger; he wanted to know why the guy hadn't married her, though it was none of his business. Regrettably, his heart didn't seem to care. He wanted to know if she was in love with the jerk.

''Grace, I—'' He couldn't tell her there hadn't been a woman who could hold a candle to her in his life. Trying again, he said, ''You're having a baby.''

''Yes. I am.'' Her stare was forthright.

''I hadn't heard you were dating anybody seriously.''

Her lips curved. ''I wasn't aware you cared what happened to anyone in Fairhaven.''

Not Cami, and certainly not me. She hadn't spoken the words, but they echoed Maggie's statement. A lot had changed in Fairhaven.

"I care. I care a lot. Right now, I care that you're expecting a baby and I don't see the proud papa hanging around."

"No. You wouldn't see him hanging around."

The sadness in her voice hurt him. She deserved better treatment than this! "Are you in love with the jerk?" he asked, hating himself for having to know.

She paused. Her lips trembled, before her lashes suddenly swept downward. "I was...once."

And then it hit him. Like a piercing flash of light in a dense fog, Brant knew why the regulars at the Yellowjacket had been staring at him. Knew what was behind Maggie's broad grin. They hadn't been waiting to rib him about his rush to Cami's defense.

"It's mine, isn't it?" he whispered hoarsely. Without waiting for her to confirm or deny it, Brant's gaze riveted back to her stomach. That was six months worth of pregnancy, at least. He remembered their last night together and the warm glow in Grace's eyes, those fascinating hazel eyes, as he'd lain with her in his bedroom. November hadn't yet brought the chill of winter, but they'd enjoyed the humid wisps of wind filtering through an open window across their skin.

That night she had mentioned marriage. He had known inside himself their relationship had to be over.

This, then, was the repayment for his reluctance. Only Grace had paid the price, alone.

"I'm so sorry," he began. "I had no—"

The shop door swung open. A tall, broad-shouldered man walked inside, his gaze immediately swinging to Brant.

"Heard you were back in town, Brant."

"Howdy, Kyle."

An unmistakable aura of uneasiness permeated the room. They formed a triangle of sorts standing there, each watching the other. Brant could feel the other man's intense dislike.

"Are you ready, Grace?" Kyle asked.

"Let me lock up." She shot a pointed glance Brant's way. He realized he was *persona non grata,* not that he'd been *grata* since he'd walked in the store.

Slinging Cami's wedding gown over one arm, he nodded briskly at Kyle. "Thanks," he said to Grace. Then he left, his blood racing with jealous unhappiness.

In the window across the street, a row of faces disappeared from sight. Brant groaned, knowing what topic was going to be discussed over pork chops and grilled onions tonight. He could hear the whispers: *If Brant hadn't been so wary of a woman wearing wedding white, he might not be watching his lady—and his baby—strolling down the street with another man.*

Impatiently Brant tossed Cami's wedding gown into the front seat next to him, furious that the errand she'd sent him on had been a ploy.

GRACE FELT Brant's hard-eyed gaze burning all the way through the back of her maternity dress as she left the store. A thousand emotions had streaked into her mind when he'd walked into the shop. Seeing him had been a shock to her senses she'd hoped she was well past. Until she had looked into his eyes, seen his tall body standing in her store, Grace had thought she was safe.

Now she knew she was anything but. The disappointment she had felt when Brant told her he was picking up Cami's wedding dress had been worse than almost anything she'd ever felt. For a second, that girlish, wistful dream had played in her mind; she actually hoped he had come into her store to tell her he wanted to be back in her life. That he missed her, missed what they'd known together.

The same fantasy had lived in her mind day after day, each one blending into another as she'd learned to exist without him. Brant's unexpected appearance had shattered those silver-edged dreams immediately. He was only doing a favor for his sister. Doubtless, without Cami's errand, Grace would never have seen Brant's boots standing on the plush, white carpet of the wedding salon.

"Are you going to be all right?" Kyle asked.

Grace shot him a bittersweet smile. "I decided I would be all right a long time ago."

He wound his arm across her back in a comforting motion. "If I can help you in any way—"

"You can't. But thank you for caring." Grace felt that was more than Brant had done. Why couldn't she love Kyle with the same hunger and passion her reckless heart wanted to give to Brant—a man who didn't want her love?

"I do more than care." His eyes conveyed his greater feelings.

Grace sighed. "I know you do. That's what makes this whole thing so sad."

He squeezed her tight as they walked, just for a moment, but long enough for Grace to appreciate the tender gesture. "I don't feel sad. I think that now that you've seen the old boyfriend, you'll decide I'm the man with the hot stuff.''

She had to laugh. "Kyle, I think I already got burned.''

"Yeah, well. Today, maybe it feels that way. After some Chinese food and jasmine tea for lunch, you'll start feeling a little better. Who knows?'' He leaned down to drop a light kiss on her forehead. "Tomorrow, maybe you don't even notice a scar.''

"I hope so.'' Grace didn't want to ever lay eyes on Brant again if it was going to hurt so bad. She had been going along just fine, adjusting to life the way it was obviously going to be, when he had strolled into her life as if nothing of any importance had ever abided between them. He hadn't so much as blinked—until he'd seen her stomach. "I think it was just the shock.'' She smiled at Kyle despite the pain. "In fact, I'm starting to feel better already.''

It was an untruth, but she had already spent too many months trying to mend her broken heart to allow it to crack again. The baby kicked suddenly, startling Grace into a distressing realization.

Whether she liked it or not, now she had to think for two.

"Uh-oh." Tilly jumped away from her spying position. "I think Brant saw us.''

Maggie stepped back from the window, too, though she knew Tilly was right. "It doesn't make any difference that he did. The shock Brant just got was about the worst a man can get. Anyway, he knows this cafe is more about talking than eating.''

"Do you think they got anything settled?'' Buzz

Jones asked. His checkers lay untouched on the board.

"Nope. Not if Grace is walking out with Kyle."

Purvis Brown rubbed his stubbled white whiskers thoughtfully. "I figured Brant would be man enough to do the right thing by Grace."

Maggie shook her head. "I don't think it has much to do with what Brant would be man enough to do at this point. He lost his chance to do much of anything."

Tilly wiped the tables with a clean rag. "I was hoping for a fairy-tale ending, though."

"Been reading too many romances," Maggie told her. "Still, I don't mind saying I was hoping Kyle would be a little late for their daily lunch outing."

"Brant did kind of skedaddle after Kyle showed up," Buzz agreed. He tapped his hand idly on the checkerboard. "Ah, well. Guess you'll still be Grace's delivery coach, Maggie."

"Yeah. Don't suppose I'll be trading my place of honor with Brant."

She sounded sad, and Tilly shook her head. "We were expecting too much too soon, maybe. They just need a little more time."

"Six months apart was probably long enough," Purvis interjected gloomily. "It was long enough for Grace to fall in love with another man."

Maggie lowered the red wooden blinds in the Yellowjacket, one by one, to block out the hot afternoon sun. "I guess we can quit waiting for double wedding announcements." She let out a heavy sigh. "Grace wouldn't still be seeing Kyle if she had any feelings left for Brant. She's gotten over the man."

Chapter Two

"Cami!"

Brant's roar and slamming of the front door shook the silk flower arrangement on its podium in the hall. He meant for his voice—and his anger—to travel all the way up the stairs. He took them two at a time.

Pounding on his sister's door, Brant let out another shout. "Don't you cower in there, Camille Durning! You dished it out, now you try taking some of it yourself!"

"Yes, brother?" Cami's voice, pitched sweetly, filtered through the door. "I'll be more than glad to take anything you care to dish out."

He opened the door, eyeing his sister with anger.

"My dress! Thank you, Brant."

She hopped out of the bed as if she were a delighted little girl. Some of his ire tried to seep out of him, but Brant told himself his sister had pulled a very disturbing trick on him. As siblings, they had enjoyed the rivalry of one-upmanship. This time, she'd gotten him fair and square—but he didn't like it one bit.

He held up a warning hand before she could reach the plastic-covered dress. "Uh-uh. We talk before you try on.'' He hung the dress on a high hook inside her closet.

"Talk about what, Brant?'' Cami's eyes were wide.

"You knew about Grace.'' When she tried to speak, he shook his head. "Don't try to deny it.''

Reddish brown curls bounced as she tossed her hair off of her shoulders. "I'm not denying it. Don't *you* try to deny that you're glad you know now, instead of waiting years to find out you had a child.''

He crossed his arms. "Did you spring that on me so I couldn't complain anymore about your unmarried state?''

Cami didn't blink. "No. I don't care how much you complain about that. I didn't ask you to see Grace to rub anything in your face. I feel sorry for you. You might marry someone else and never know what a mistake you had made. Now, there's still time.''

Brant's mouth dropped. Marry someone else? For heaven's sake, he hadn't even been able to marry Grace. What made Cami think he might marry someone else? The memory of Grace walking down the street with Kyle beside her shot through him with a dark, disquieting pain. *Grace* might marry someone else, though, who would raise *Brant's* child. The prospect of that made Brant feel ill. "You could have warned me.''

She shook her head, crossing to examine the pearls on her wedding gown with a lustrous smile. "It wasn't my place. If Grace had never hunted you down to tell you, then she didn't want you to know. For whatever reason.''

For whatever reason. Oh, he knew what the reason

was. Their breakup had been difficult, to say the very least, for both of them. It had been the hardest thing he'd ever done. Now, he wished he hadn't quite burned his bridge behind him. "She appears to be pretty tight with Kyle Macaffee."

Cami didn't look away from her dress. Instead she pulled the plastic up over it and began undoing the pearl buttons in back. "Did you think no one else was going to want her?"

"No." The word felt like a growl. "But not with my child."

Now she did look at him. "Well, there's the problem. You have a medieval thought process warring with a modern-day woman. It's going to be difficult to sort that out." Cami hesitated, before reaching out to tap his forehead with her finger. "You'd better start working on it. It'll probably take you a while."

Brant didn't appreciate that. "There was more wrong with our relationship than my medieval thought processes, Cami."

She sighed, pointing her finger toward the doorway, indicating that he should leave. Obviously she was dying to try on that dress.

"Brant, think about why you wouldn't marry her. Think about why it's bothering you now. Then go back and get my veil, please? I won't be a proper bride without my veil."

"Your veil! Camille Durning, I'm not going back to the Wedding Wonderland for a damn thing! This time, you do the fetching."

He stalked out, narrowly avoiding slamming the bedroom door behind him. When had his sister turned into such a fountain of wisdom? It was irritating as hell.

More irritating than anything, though, was the fact that in the shock of seeing Grace, he hadn't paid the balance on the wedding gown. He could call her and get the amount and send it in. He could make Cami find out, since it was her gown, anyway.

The problem was, he really needed to speak to Grace, ornery and thorny as she was going to be with him. The veil and the balance of the bill would give him an excuse to see her.

Then maybe he could start figuring out what the hell to do about the mess he'd gotten himself into. Tomorrow, he told himself, he would make another trip to the Wedding Wonderland.

BRANT WOKE UP at two o'clock in the morning, realizing he'd never really done more than doze. The fact that the only woman he had ever cared deeply about was carrying his child was killing him. His stomach hurt. His head felt as if baseballs were rolling around inside it. Even his teeth hurt from grinding them.

He had to talk to her. In the light of day, across from the Yellowjacket Cafe, just wouldn't do. Brant pulled on jeans and a fairly wrinkled denim shirt, stuffed his feet into some boots and made a cursory effort at tooth and hair brushing. None of this grooming was going to matter if he couldn't get Grace to open her front door.

Driving across town, Brant used the time to mull over whether he was making a smart move. Damn it, he should have told Kyle to take a hike today and dragged Grace off to discuss what they were going to do about her problem. *His* problem, too, now.

Turning off the headlights, Brant pulled his truck

into the gravel driveway in front of Grace's house. She lived in an old, wood frame house, circa the early 1900s. Her business was a block away, and she liked to walk the short distance. He wondered if she still did that, in her condition. With a snort, Brant eyed the dark house, knowing that if he so much as tried to inquire after Grace's exercise habits right now, she'd tell him what road to take to the highway.

Getting out of the truck, he quietly shut the door. Crickets chirped in the early May morning, a sound he normally found soothing but which tonight was as loud and irritating as the beating of his heart. He thought about Grace sleeping upstairs in her bed, with all its lacy white ruffles hanging down from the canopy and his heart clenched in a spasm his groin recognized. He thought about her waking up, softly tousled and warm from the heaping of covers she loved, and decided it was a bad idea to ring the doorbell. He told himself it was a bad idea for her to walk down those wooden stairs in a sleepy state, where she might lose her balance and fall. The truth was, he didn't think he could stand so close to her, see her in her nightwear, and do much serious talking.

Picking up a handful of the tiniest gravel he could find, Brant aimed one pebble at Grace's window. Another one followed before he saw the curtains pull back hesitantly. Firing one last missile, he was glad to see the lamp beside her bed switch on. The window protested a bit as she raised it. Brant told himself that was something he would fix one day.

"Brant! What are you doing out there?"

"I need to talk to you, Grace."

"Talk! I have nothing to talk to you about, especially not at this hour."

"Grace, we have to get some things resolved!"

"Brant, listen. Six months ago, you needed to resolve some things. I didn't. Not then, and not now."

He wasn't getting very far with her. Frankly he hadn't really expected to. "I won't claim we parted on the best of terms, Grace. But don't you think you owed it to me to tell me you were pregnant?"

Her hesitation gave her away. Her words, flat as a steel-edge, did not. "I don't owe you a thing."

"We owe it to the child you're carrying to make some responsible decisions."

Grace leaned out the window a little farther, as if she couldn't believe what she was hearing. "Pardon me? Is this the same man who didn't want anything to do with responsibilities? The same man who went off and left his sister to run the family ranch?"

Brant took both those barbs with a sigh. "Grace, I made some mistakes. I wasn't ready to face some things. But is keeping me away from my child the answer?"

She shook her head, making the fall of long blond hair wave gently. "I haven't admitted this is your child."

"Give me a break. Everybody in this town knows it is. They'll put my name on the birth certificate in the Father blank no matter what you tell them. All I want is a chance to share in this with you."

"Share what, Brant? The morning sickness? That's been a treat, as I'm sure Cami can tell you. The water retention, sore breasts? Stray aches and pains that keep me up at night? Which of those did you want to share?"

He ran a hand across his chin. There wasn't anything he could do to alleviate those things she was suffering. But he could help her out financially.

"I'd like to see that you and the baby are taken care of."

The slamming of the window was like a rifle shot through the quiet countryside.

"Damn it!" Brant leaned down, scooped up some more gravel and flung it at her window.

Instantly headlights were turned on him. Brant jerked around, realizing immediately that their heated discussion had kept him from noticing the sheriff's cruiser pulling up next to the curb. The sheriff had flipped on the headlights of Brant's truck, and now Brant was glaringly exposed.

"Evening, Brant," Sheriff Farley said easily. "Or should I say good morning?"

Brant held back a groan of embarrassment. John Farley dated Maggie at the Yellowjacket Cafe. Well, he dated her as much as he'd ever dated anyone. It was a similarity Brant and the sheriff had in common: an ambitious desire to avoid the altar. As much as he recognized another male who would probably take his side, Brant also knew John wouldn't be able to resist mentioning this early-morning visit to Maggie.

"Something I can help you with?" John asked.

"Hell, no," Brant grumbled.

"Woman trouble's a drag, isn't it?" The sheriff's hearty laugh echoed in the night. Brant pushed back his irritation. "Still, it's a bit early for you to be trying to get on Grace's good side, isn't it?"

On cue, the window slid back up.

"This gentleman bothering you, Grace?"

She paused before answering, "As much as he ever has. Did somebody call you out?"

"Nope. I was just driving by when I spotted a truck in your driveway. Couldn't recall any truck being parked here at night before, so I thought I'd check."

Not Brant's truck, but not Kyle's, either. Brant took that as a reassuring piece of information.

"At least you're doing your job, Sheriff." Grace's voice lacked the humiliation Brant was feeling. There wasn't a prayer John wouldn't mention this episode to Maggie. By morning, he was going to be in worse shape for gossip than if he'd merely had a limo filled with doves pull up in front of the Wedding Wonderland.

"By the way, when are you going to let me fit you for a tux, John?"

"For Cami's wedding?"

"For yours." Her tone was only slightly teasing. "I can't help noticing that gleam in your eye every time you look at Miss Maggie."

That got the sheriff heading back toward his cruiser. "I'll let you know when it becomes absolutely necessary, Grace. Sorry to have disturbed your, um, conversation, Brant."

"That's all right, John. As Grace said, it's nice to know the county's safe."

John tossed a sarcastic wave-off back his way. Brant snorted, then glanced back up at Grace. She was staring at him, her eyes huge with some emotion. He couldn't help noticing the way her nightgown collar fluttered in the slight breeze, and the fact that she looked more beautiful than ever.

"I guess I'll go now, seeing as how I've given people something to talk about."

"When are you going to stop worrying about what everybody thinks, Brant? When are you going to start doing what you feel is right?"

He stopped, half turned. "What the hell's that supposed to mean? You don't mind being the topic of conversation at everybody's breakfast table?"

"Would I be pregnant and unmarried if I did?" she shot back. "Just once, if you could see that those same gossips are good-hearted, that they're friends, you might be able to relax enough to appreciate them. John, for instance, wasn't just driving by here randomly. Ever since you left, and Maggie told him I was expecting, he's been coming down my street. He hasn't told me that. Maggie told me he was doing it. That makes me feel awfully good that someone in this town cares about me enough to go out of his way."

"Like Kyle?" The minute it was out of his mouth, Brant realized how dumb he sounded. How eaten up with jealousy.

Which he was.

"I'm going to ignore that for now. I know you're all bothered because John knows you were here and will probably say so to Maggie." She shook a finger at him. "Maggie has lunch sent over to me when I have girls come in who need to be fitted on their lunch hour. There's usually a warm biscuit, maybe some orange juice sent over with Tilly in the morning, always saying they had leftovers. It's not true.

They're worried about me. They're trying their best to take care of me."

"Because I'm not."

"You said it, not me. But just for the record, let me say that I didn't give myself to you so that I'd have someone to take care of me."

"I know that." Brant sighed, shaking his head. He was making a huge mess of this again. "Grace, will you at least give my offer some thought? I know I'm not putting it as pretty as it should be, but I honestly want to provide for my child. And the least I can do is help you with your medical expenses."

"Would that ease your conscience, Brant? Would that make you feel less like the villain in everybody's opinion?"

Was that what it looked like he was trying to do? Weigh the balance of public opinion in his favor by offering to do his financial and emotional share of what she was going through? "I don't know what you want me to say, Grace."

The time she took to consider his words seemed forever. Finally she, too, sighed, as he had. "I don't know, either, Brant. Maybe you're being more honest than I am."

Quietly, this time, Grace slid the window shut. The lamplight flicked off. Brant was left in the dark, the chirping of the crickets the only noise in the damning silence.

AFTER A NIGHT OF TOSSING and turning, Brant got up, noticing the time was an hour past his normal time to awaken. Pulling on work clothes, he decided he felt worse this morning than he ever had with a hangover.

Downstairs, the kitchen lights were on. Coffee perked in the coffeemaker, and there was a mug sitting out with his name on it. Brant filled the mug, nearly dropping it when the back door opened.

"What are you doing?" he roared at Cami.

His sister pulled off her boots, laying them on the porch as she shot him an arch look. "What does it look like?"

"Like you've been out feeding the cows!"

"I have been." She crossed to fill her coffee mug again. "Did you want them to go hungry?"

"Hell, no. I was going out to do it."

Cami shrugged. "Sorry. Force of habit."

She hadn't said it, but the implication was there. *I kept this place running while you were gone.* He didn't feel that she blamed him for anything, simply that she wanted him to understand that she'd gotten along fine without him and could again if necessary.

Cami was a lot like Grace, he realized.

"How's the morning sickness?" he asked gruffly.

"Not bad enough to keep me from doing chores." She sat down at the table and peeled a banana. "Although, I will admit that I don't eat breakfast before I go out and I try hard to be extremely fast about the chores. I've had a bout or two with some sympathetic cows looking on." Shooting him a smile, she said, "However, I think I'm over all that."

He grunted. "You've made a fast recovery since yesterday."

"Yes. Well, did you get my veil?" she asked brightly.

His attention was caught by the grin on Cami's face. "How would I have done that?"

"I thought maybe you picked it up when you left at two o'clock this morning."

"No." He shook his head. "I did not get your veil."

"Oh. I guess I didn't really expect that you had."

He could tell she hadn't by the teasing tone of her voice. "You're so recovered I imagine you can get it yourself today. And pay the balance of the bill."

"Whew! Didn't go well with Grace, huh?"

Brant resisted slamming his palm on the kitchen counter. He settled for a glare at his sister. "Did anyone ever tell you to mind your own business, Cami?"

"Oh, this from the lone ranger who was prepared to blow the doors off my fiancé's house."

Sighing, he sat down across from his sister. "No. I didn't get far at all. I don't know what I'm supposed to say to her, and I end up saying all the wrong things."

"Hmm. A case of foot-in-mouth disease. There's only one cure for that."

"What the hell would that be?" Brant eyed his sister suspiciously.

"You have to learn to like the taste of your own foot."

"Very funny."

Cami laughed, giving him a playful slap on the forearm. "Oh, Brant. What do you expect Grace to do? Greet you with open arms? She has a right to be ticked.''

"Is she ticked? Is this something she'll get over if I keep seeing her?''

"Well, no.'' The smile left Cami's face and she considered her words carefully. "I mean, yes, she is angry. She isn't going to let you back into her life without knowing what part you want to play in it.''

"I offered financial and emotional support.''

"And?''

"And what?''

"And what else?''

Brant drew his brows together, having a funny feeling he knew where Cami was going to head with this one.

"Did you say anything about your feelings for her?''

No, he hadn't. "Um, no.''

"Then I guess you're lucky you got her to even come to the door at that hour. You're even more fortunate she didn't fire a shotgun at you. Did it ever occur to you to say something more feeling than 'hey, I'll pick up the tab'?''

"I might have gotten around to it if the sheriff hadn't thought I was a trespasser.''

"John was there?''

"Yeah.'' Brant hated to have to admit that.

"Oh, boy.'' Cami was silent for a moment. "Listen, Brant, you're going to have to hurry and fix this thing right. No more of your delaying tactics.''

"Delaying tactics! What the hell's that supposed to mean?''

"You don't have time to keep making Grace mad with offers to support her. She doesn't need your support. She owns the only wedding shop in Fairhaven and gets more business than she can handle. Besides, she wouldn't marry you for economic reasons, anyway."

"Whoa. Hang on a minute. Nobody said anything about marriage."

"You're not going to marry Grace?" Cami's eyes were huge.

"I think we established that six months ago." Brant felt mutinous on this matter. Yes, the gossip was going to be uncomfortable. The situation was awkward. They had always been careful about birth control, but the fact that something had gone awry didn't change his mind about bachelorhood. He sighed raggedly. Why couldn't Grace have been content knowing she was the only woman he'd ever given as much of himself to as he had?

"Brant, do you think you're letting our parents' divorce affect you just a little too much?"

He stared at his sister, suddenly angry. "*Do not* bring that up to me."

"You can't talk to me that way, Brant. I think your fear is due to what happened between Mom and Dad."

"I think you still haven't outgrown your mouth," he growled.

She shrugged. "Fine. Ignore it if you want. You're going to keep paying for it as long as you do."

"Cami, be quiet." His tone brooked no argument.

Without acknowledging his command, Cami said,

''By the way, Brant, I need you to sign over half the ranch acreage to me.''

''What?''

''It's half mine. I'm taking it with me when I get married.''

''Damn nice dowry,'' he grumbled. ''Leaves me with only a thousand acres.''

''Yes. Well, I don't feel too guilty about that since you left me to take care of all of it while you were trying to get over Grace.'' Cami stood. ''If I were you, I'd try to spend some time thinking about what you're going to say to Grace when you see her next, Brant. Much as you can be a stubborn old mule, I hate to think of you sitting on the porch alone at night, with an empty house your only reward for your insecurity.''

''Cami!'' This time, Brant did slam his palm against the table.

''Have the fence line moved, please, Brant. Maybe it will start you thinking about what life's going to be like when I'm gone.''

She sailed out of the kitchen. Brant heard her running up the stairs. Muttering a string of curses to himself, he went out the front door. Heading to the mailboxes at the end of the road, Brant halted in his quest for the morning newspaper. A truck was pulling up the long driveway, a truck he recognized since he'd helped her pick it out. Brant's stomach pitched.

It stopped beside him. ''Is this a payback for my unannounced visit last night?'' he asked, trying to sound as if his heart hadn't plummeted into his boots.

''At least you're not in your nightgown,'' Grace

returned lightly. "Is Cami in from feeding the live-stock?"

"Yeah."

"Thanks." The truck roared off, kicking up white dust around him. She hadn't come to see him at all, Brant realized with a sense of letdown. "Is Cami in from feeding the livestock?" he mimicked under his breath. Deciding the paper could wait, Brant headed back to the house. Hell, Cami had already pried a thousand acres out of him. With those two putting their heads together, he might find himself without a house, too, if he wasn't there to protect what was his.

Worse, he might find himself on the opposite end of the shotgun he'd been prepared to use on Cami's fiancé.

Chapter Three

Grace put the veil gently on top of Cami's hair, brushing the burnished waves into a tamer look. "There. It suits you perfectly."

"It's beautiful, Grace. I should have known to trust your judgment."

The illusion veil was simple, with an unpretentious pearl band that set off the color of Cami's hair. Grace had argued in favor of this look, while Cami had selected a taller, more elaborate headdress, wanting the appearance of height as she stood next to her handsome groom. Grace had known this was the right look for Cami. The look was understated and beautiful, just the way a woman should look on her wedding day.

"Well, I was just afraid the other veil was going to overpower you," Grace said. "I'm glad you're happy."

Cami hugged her. "I'm sorry you had to bring it out."

"I didn't mind." Grace began closing the makeup bag, which held hairpins and other things a bride might require. "Your brother suffered so much coming into my shop yesterday I couldn't put him through that misery again.''

''Brant's misery is his own.''

''Yes.'' Grace gave a shrug she really didn't mean. ''Still, my running this out here gave me a chance to spend a moment with you privately. Cami, there's something I want to talk to you about.''

Cami turned interested eyes on her. ''Okay.''

''Kyle Macaffee has asked me to marry him.''

''Oh.''

''I'm considering his offer.''

''Oh!'' Cami's eyes grew wide.

''The only reason I'm telling you this is because I want you to understand. Your brother and I didn't have what it took to make a lifetime of commitment to each other. Kyle loves me...well, just for me.''

''Do you love him?''

Grace paused. The answer was so difficult. ''Not with the raging, out-of-control passion I felt for Brant, perhaps. But what I have with Kyle feels solid, much more lasting, somehow.''

''I see.'' Cami's tone was quiet.

''I hope you do. I know you had hopes that Brant and I would...well, never mind. Suffice to say that doesn't matter now.'' She sighed, feeling despondent as she snapped her purse closed. ''I don't know what my answer to Kyle will be, yet. I need more time to think, to think about my baby, especially. But I wanted you to know, just in case I decide to accept his proposal.''

''Thank you for telling me,'' Cami murmured, her eyes downcast. ''You deserve a good man, Grace.''

''There's a favor I hate to ask you, but I must,''

Grace continued. "Please don't mention this to your brother."

"Oh, Grace, don't ask that of me!"

She held up a hand. "Please, Cami. My life has gone on. I don't want your brother running back into it and hurting me in any way. He…simply isn't capable of loving me the way I want to be loved, and—" Her words broke off. "I just don't need any more complications right now. You understand that, don't you?"

Cami nodded, her expression unhappy. "I hate to say it, but I do. I won't mention Kyle's proposal to Brant."

Grace hugged the woman she had once hoped would become her sister-in-law. Always she had thought of Cami as a sister. Her and Brant's situation was going to hurt Cami, Grace knew. But there wasn't anything she could do about that—except be honest. She had decided after Brant's visit last night that perhaps she wasn't being honest with herself. Or anyone else, with her brave attitude. She really wasn't so brave inside, not since she'd seen Brant.

She really was still hanging on to hope. All that was going to bring her was a broken heart—again.

"Thanks, Cami." Pulling away, Grace gave her a watery smile. "Your wedding is going to be beautiful."

"At least you're going to be my maid of honor," Cami sniffled. "We'll be in one wedding together."

"Yes." Grace picked up her things and went to the door. "Can you meet me for lunch today at the Yellowjacket after church? There's something Maggie and Tilly and I want to talk to you about."

"That sounds wonderful. I could use some home cooking."

"Me, too. See you then." Grace went out the door, waving Cami back when she would have followed her downstairs to the door. The quieter her exit, the better. She didn't want to run the risk of running into Brant.

But he was sitting inside her truck in the passenger seat, his Stetson pulled down over his eyes and his arms crossed. Grace's heartbeat picked up.

"What do you think you're doing?" she demanded as she reached the car window.

He pushed the hat brim back. "Waiting to talk to you."

"You couldn't do that inside?"

"Didn't want to miss you in case you tried to leave without saying goodbye."

Grace's eyes met his guiltily. "I wouldn't have done that."

"Oh. You looked for me, then."

"Well, maybe not directly—"

"Ah. I see."

They were silent for a moment. "As I mentioned last night," Grace finally said, "I don't feel any great need to talk to you."

"Did Cami pay you?"

"No, but I'll send you a bill. That's not why you're occupying space in my truck. Don't beat around the bush. This is my only day off, and I'd like to make it to church on time."

"I'm sitting in here because you're a captive audience this way. Would you have come and sat down in my den to drink a glass of tea and talk about what

we're going to do with our lives if I'd asked you?''
Brant quirked a questioning brow at her.

"No."

"Figured as much. I take it you didn't like my offer last night."

Grace shook her head, wishing she still wasn't attracted to Brant's dark handsomeness. It made everything so much more difficult. "I don't need your money, Brant. I wasn't in it for that. And I've been taking care of myself for six months now. I bet I can make it through everything else without you."

"And my baby? Does it have to learn to live without me, too?"

"I think your son will do just fine."

"Son?" Brant sat straight up in his seat.

Grace wondered why men always perked up at the mention of a son. "Maybe it's a daughter." Grace fibbed, just to rattle him.

"Daughter?" Brant's posture didn't relax. "Have you decided what to name her?"

She sighed, realizing either gender tag seemed to have an electrifying result on him. The man might be immune to matrimony, but the idea of being a father seemed to have an astonishing effect on him. He almost sounded as if he could make a commitment to the infant growing inside her.

"It's a boy." Grace decided to give in on this issue. He was going to find out sooner or later, anyway. "I haven't picked out a name."

"Do you have a good doctor?"

"I'm seeing the new guy in town. He seems fairly astute. Actually he's been pretty helpful." Grace hadn't wanted to drive all the way into Dallas, so she'd gone to check out the man who'd taken old

Dr. Watkins place in the town clinic. So far, Dr. Brig Delancey had proved helpful and encouraging.

"I don't like new guys."

A little stiffness left Grace. She had felt the same way. "I don't usually trust newcomers myself. Especially with my baby. But I like him. I really do. Though I still miss Dr. Watkins."

"Yeah." Brant's eyes shadowed. "Grace, let me help you out with this."

She looked down at her Sunday dress boots, wishing with all her heart she could let him. Unfortunately, letting Brant hang around and do the expectant father routine would put her through an emotional wringer. She didn't plan on keeping him from his child, but she didn't want to be shredded by unrequited love when she needed so badly to stay strong.

"I can't, Brant." She lifted her gaze to meet his eyes. "I've come too far on my own. Please understand."

He was silent for a long moment, before getting out of the truck. Shutting the door, he walked around the front to her side. "Let me know if you need anything?"

"I will." She knew he would be the last person she would call for help.

His finger grazed her chin lightly. "I have so many different thoughts running around inside my head about this I can't begin to think of the right thing to say to you. But I'm not through trying to talk you into letting me help you."

Grace stepped away, opening the door to get inside the truck. She felt much safer behind a closed door. Putting her bag and purse on the seat beside her, she started the engine. With one last glance Brant's way, Grace reversed the truck, making a semicircle, before she drove back up the driveway.

Brant didn't understand that she didn't need the kind of help he was offering. Once, she had needed something more, something he couldn't give her, which was why their relationship hadn't worked out in the first place. Tears blurred her eyes. The most devastating part was how much remembering made her ache. She still wanted everything she'd wanted before.

A SON. Brant couldn't help the grin on his face. He was going to have a little boy, a little Brant Durning, Junior. The thought was incredible. Up until the moment Grace had said that, he had thought of the life growing inside her as a sort of thing, a responsibility he needed to shoulder. Now the reality of it had hit him, with all the accompanying excitement.

He was going to have a boy.

Going inside the house, Brant hardly noticed his sister standing in the hallway staring at him. "Did Grace have a change of heart? Or you?" she asked.

Startled out of his daydream, he turned to look at his sister. "What are you asking me?"

"Um, maybe why you've got that goofy smile on your face?"

Pausing, Brant didn't even bother to counteract his sister's crafty barb. "I'm going to have a son," he told her.

"I'm going to be an aunt to a little boy?" Cami's grin was huge.

"Didn't Grace tell you?"

She shook her head. "Not that. I can't believe it.

I'm going to start crocheting a blue baby afghan. With some white stripes running through it. Or maybe orange and white, for our high school spirit colors. I'll have to ask Grace what color the nursery is going to be.''

Cami walked away, lost in her plans. Brant stared after her, still grinning. He felt lost between a desire to give a victory shout or rub his hands as if he were a little kid getting a favorite toy. In the end, he did both, thinking about how beautiful Grace looked in the lace and denim maternity dress that had flowed around her short boots.

Heckfire. She was having his son.

THE YELLOWJACKET was crowded, per usual for a Sunday lunch crowd. That suited Grace just fine. Her meeting with Tilly, Maggie and Cami would go much better if they didn't have a chance to talk too intimately. The last thing she wanted to be asked about was her pregnancy, or her lunch date yesterday with Kyle. Today should be Cami's day. After all, she was getting married in two short weeks.

Grace was not. She pushed aside the slight tingle of envy she felt for her unmarried state. It was a status she had chosen, by not telling Brant in the first place that she was pregnant. Oh, he might not have asked her to marry him even then. It had been a gamble on her part. Having taken a home pregnancy test—one that the pharmacist had sworn was as reliable as any test in a doctor's office—Grace had lightly questioned Brant about marriage. If he had responded positively to her question, she would have mentioned the pregnancy. His vehemently negative reaction had stunned her and she hadn't wanted to compound the error by telling him they were going to have a baby. He would only have resented her for feeling as if he had to marry her. She would always have known, in her heart.

Before she had begun to show, he had left Fairhaven for three long months. His desertion had forced her to realize their relationship was truly over. He didn't miss her, didn't plan on reuniting. She had been frightened, then, knowing her condition would soon make its own blatant announcement. So she had opted for a straightforward approach in telling her friends. To her surprise, her admission had sat very well with the folks she had known all her life: Maggie, Sheriff Farley, Buzz, Purvis, Tilly and others. It had all worked out for her.

But today was Cami's day. She couldn't help being glad that she and Cami would be forever connected to each other by blood, anyway, no matter that they would never be true in-laws.

Cami came in, her lustrous sable hair glowing in the afternoon sunlight. Grace waved her over to the table.

"You look better than you did this morning," she told her. "A shower really does do wonders, doesn't it?"

Cami laughed. "Yes. Early-morning cattle feeding doesn't do much for my looks."

"I believe I've felt that way after sitting up late a few nights making adjustments to wedding gowns for nervous brides." Grace smiled as Tilly and Maggie came over to sit with them.

"Thanks for coming, Cami. We've got to make this quick, because the kitchen won't last long without us, I'm afraid. We wanted to ask you in person, honey.'' Maggie paused, her brown eyes alight with friendly caring. ''Would you let the three of us throw you a wedding shower? A real, honest-to-goodness wedding shower, catered by Tilly and me?''

''Oh.'' Cami's eyes misted over as she looked around the table at her friends. ''That would be lovely. But you're already doing my wedding buffet, Maggie. Isn't that too much?''

''Nope. Believe me, some folks in this town have been awful glad to get the extra employment. We were so worried you'd take your business into Dallas, Cami.''

''No way. Everything I've always wanted is right here in Fairhaven.'' She smiled around the table.

That was a stark contrast to the wandering foot Cami's brother had. Everything Brant had ever wanted was certainly not in Fairhaven. She'd expected him to come home from college with a serious girlfriend. When he'd first asked her out, Grace had thought he was joking. The second time he asked her out, Grace wondered what he saw in her. By the time they started making love, she thought the best thing that could have happened to her was Brant being in her life.

Not any more permanently than anything else in his life, though. Grace forced herself to smile Cami's way. ''We were hoping you'd let us. It was Maggie's idea to give you a shower of some kind. Traditionally I suppose we should give you a bachelorette shower, but a fancy wedding shower sounded so much more, I don't know, festive or something.''

''It does,'' Cami agreed.

''Or if you'd prefer, we could do a barbecue, and invite men and women.''

"Hmm. Would that keep the boys from dragging my fiancé into Dallas to hit the topless bars?"

"No." Maggie shook her head. "But at least we'd be together for one night with the menfolk."

"Might not be as stuffy a party, either," Tilly added. "Men tend to look forward to a barbecue."

"It's all that male-bonding as they stand around the grill." Grace's voice was wry. "But we'll be happy to do either one, Cami. We just want to do something for you."

"They both sound wonderful," Cami said slowly. "But—"

"Grim-faced rancher at three o'clock," Maggie murmured. "Don't look, but Brant's coming our way."

Grace's gaze skittered toward the door before she could stop it. The calm she'd been feeling a moment ago evaporated.

Without asking, he pulled out a chair. "Howdy, ladies."

"Howdy, Brant. What's happening with you?" Maggie asked.

"Not much. What are you ladies cooking up?"

"A bridal shower," Tilly told him.

"A bridal shower?" His stare was directed at Grace.

"Yes. We thought we'd give Cami one, since she is getting married, Brant." Grace's tone was dry. Had he looked alarmed? As in, thinking *she* was getting married? She glanced at Cami, but the other woman's face was guiltless. Cami had said she wouldn't mention Kyle's proposal, and Grace knew she wouldn't.

"Oh. Don't guess that's much of my concern,"

Brant said. "But it's nice of you to do that for Cami."

"That makes up my mind. I want the barbecue," Cami said decisively.

"What makes up your mind? What did I say?" Brant asked.

The four women stared at him. "If I have a standard ladies-only shower, the menfolk won't be interested. They'll look at the china and place mats and bud vases I get and smile condescendingly. But a barbecue will be different." She leaned over to kiss her brother's cheek. "Thanks, Brant. You are good for something."

"Don't know what that's supposed to mean," he grumbled good-naturedly.

"Well, I guess I better get back to the kitchen." Maggie stood, with Tilly following suit. "Can I get you something to eat, Brant?"

"I wasn't going to eat, but—" He looked at Grace, her expression bland as she stared at him. "I guess I could sit here and make it a threesome."

"We haven't invited you," Cami said pointedly.

"May I please join you for lunch?" Brant growled. Grace enjoyed his humbled expression, though she wasn't buying it for a minute.

"Do you mind, Grace? My big, rather bearish brother wants to eat with us."

"I don't mind." She shook her head, but the truth was, her heart was beating inside her as if it were a big drum. It felt as if everyone in the Yellowjacket Cafe could see her emotions clearly written across her face.

"What are you doing here, anyway, Brant?"

"Looking for you. Fortunately you left a note tell-

ing me where you were going, because your fiancé
called. He's not going to make it in tonight.''

"Oh, no." Cami looked stricken. "I've been
counting the minutes until he returned. What did he
say was wrong?''

"Something about the horse buying trip not wind-
ing up the way he and his father had planned. He'll
definitely be home tomorrow.''

Grace noticed how Brant's eyes skimmed his sister's face. He was completely concerned for her happiness. She thought it was nice that he'd driven in to
town to let her know. Cami would have been so disappointed if she had hurried home to get gussied up
only to discover it was all for nothing.

"Well, he'll just have to hear about the barbecue
tomorrow," Cami said, though she still sounded unhappy.

"He said he'd try to call you tonight."

Brant picked up a pretzel, his gaze swiveling to
Grace's. She started, not expecting him to catch her
watching him. Carefully she broke eye contact and
looked around the room.

Purvis and Buzz were in their usual places, red
and black checkers occupying various squares. Sheriff Farley was behind the short-order line, working a
smile out of a busy Maggie. Tilly was hurrying from
table to table with a tea pitcher. Everyone seemed to
have a purpose in life in Fairhaven. Why did Brant
find it so empty?

"Mind if I horn in?''

Grace glanced up at the sound of Kyle Macaffee's
voice.

"Would it matter if we did?" Brant asked sourly.

Grace saw the dark look Cami shot her brother.

"We'd be happy for someone to make a fourth," she said quickly. "Please sit down."

Tilly brought menus, though they all knew the fare by heart. They put in orders, then the conversation ceased at their table. Grace tried desperately to think of something to say. She felt very peculiar sitting between the man whose child she carried and the man whose marriage proposal she was considering.

"So, Macaffee," Brant said.

"Durning," Kyle said equitably.

Tilly set glasses of water and tea on the table. Grace caught Brant looking at her, and for a moment, she felt unreasonably jealous. Tilly was so attractive, and she was just like Brant. They had similar care-free, don't-tie-me-down outlooks on life. She envisioned Tilly in Brant's arms and felt a little queasy.

"Are you feeling all right, Grace?" Brant asked.

"I'm fine," she murmured. But she couldn't meet his eyes. Instead she looked at Kyle. "Did you get any sick-animal calls this weekend?"

"Would you believe I didn't get a one? This is the most quiet weekend I've had since last fall. It was kind of nice, actually." He patted Grace on the back, his hand lingering just a moment. "You know, you look a little peaked, Grace. Are you sure you're all right?"

With everyone's eyes at the table on her, Grace thought she'd never felt more humiliated. "I'm just a little warm," she said, drinking from the cool tea glass. The truth was, sitting with Kyle and Brant was indescribable torture. The baby kicked, sending her hand to her abdomen in surprise. Was he feeling his mother's distress? Kyle's hand rubbed soothingly along her back, but Grace couldn't relax. How could she sit and pretend everything was fine and dandy when she felt so pulled sitting with two men who each had a claim of sorts on her?

"You know, I think I'll go on home." Slowly Grace stood, pulling her purse to her side. "I'll feel better after I change out of my clothes, I think."

"Grace, let me walk you home," Cami offered, quick to her feet.

Thankful it was Cami who was offering, Grace nodded. "If you don't mind having to leave lunch with these two gentlemen."

Cami sent a smile Kyle's way as he stood, along with Brant. "Maybe we can do this another time, Kyle."

"I'll call you later and check on you, Grace," Kyle said.

"Thank you." She sent a grateful look his way. "I'm sure I'll be fine." Hardly sparing a glance for Brant, Grace nodded a curt goodbye before walking outside. The May heat beating down from the sky felt like hot irons. She didn't say much to Cami, who was silent herself. Grace treasured that. Probably only another pregnant woman could understand the sudden twinges that twisted inside a body stretched out of shape by a baby.

But once she got to her street, Grace noted an instant lifting of her spirits. The tree-shrouded front yard always brought her a sense of comfort. Unlocking the front door, she went inside the house, with Cami on her heels.

"I'm going to go change," she murmured.

"I'll help myself to a glass of tea from the kitchen, and if you don't mind, I'm going to put my feet up on your sofa in the parlor," Cami told her. "Just call down to me if you need anything, or if you feel so much better you want me to take off.''

"Thanks, Cami." She offered her a wan smile before heading up the stairs. Slipping off her dress and boots, Grace put on a T-shirt that reached her knees. Just doing that made her feel like a new woman. The strange feeling that had assailed her was already gone.

"I'm okay, Cami. I just needed to get out of my panty hose, I guess," she called down the stairs.

"You're sure?"

"I'm sure. Thanks."

"Okay. I'm going to take my tea with me, but I'll put it in a plastic cup."

"That's fine. Sorry about lunch."

"No problem. I'll lock the door behind me so you don't have to come down."

Cami's voice filtered away. Grace went back into her room, seeking the comfort of her bed. Lying down, she wiggled her toes and tried not to lay on her back squarely. The doctor had said it was best in the later stages of pregnancy to rotate sides, thereby keeping pressure off the main artery in the back. He had also said she should get lots of rest, but Grace found it difficult to do that. No wonder she was feeling a bit run-down. It was her only day off, and all she had done today was keep busy.

But staying busy kept her from brooding, Grace thought as she closed her eyes. It wasn't healthy for the baby to have an unhappy mother; he would sense it. She would be happy and serene for her baby's sake—which meant staying out of Brant's path as much as possible.

DOWNSTAIRS, Cami and Brant were engaged in a heated, though whispered, argument.

"I can't leave you in here with her! Grace would kill me!"

Brant shook his head, determined. Placing the sack containing the lunch Grace had ordered in the refrigerator, he said, "I'll just watch TV until she awakens. She worried me with that sick look she had."

He had never thought it was possible for a person to go so white. Grace had done more than worry him. She had nearly gotten herself a trip over to the new doc's office.

"She's going to be furious with me," Cami moaned. "Don't touch her, or upset her at all!" she commanded. "I think the reason she looked so ill was having to sit between the two men in her life!"

Cami clapped a hand over her mouth. Brant's warning sensors picked up. "Are you hiding something from me?"

"No." Cami's face was stricken. "Brant, do not so much as say or do a thing to upset that poor woman up there. I really think she's been through enough." She gave him a narrow look. "In fact, I'm not sure I shouldn't stay with you in a chaperon capacity."

"I am only staying until I'm certain she's fine," Brant said. "I'm not the big bad wolf."

"I'm not so certain," Cami grumbled. "I'm also not certain Grace isn't going to have my head for this." She shot her brother a last suspicious glare. "You're not doing this to get one up on Kyle, are you?"

"Do I need to?" Brant eyed Cami. She definitely was hiding something.

''You might need to. Whether or not you can, I don't know.'' Cami stared up at the ceiling. ''Grace is resting. She needs it. Please don't do anything to make me regret this.''

''I won't. I swear.''

Brant shooed his sister out the door. With one last uncertain look at him, Cami headed off. The house was quiet and still after he closed the door. From the dining room window, he watched her walk down the street, heading toward the Yellowjacket where she would pick up her truck. Five minutes later, when he was very sure Cami wouldn't have second thoughts about his intentions, Brant locked the door.

Very quietly, he ascended the stairs.

Chapter Four

Brant couldn't resist a small glance in on Grace. It couldn't hurt anything to check on her. He would look in her room so fast, it would really just be a blur to salve his concern.

Walking from the stairwell across to her bedroom, Brant's eyes riveted to Grace as she lay in the white canopied bed. She looked like an angel. His breath caught in his chest as his gaze slid from her blond hair ruffling gently across the pillow, to the one slender, bare leg she had curled up over the covers.

Her stomach wasn't obvious as she lay on her side, hidden by the blanket. Still, Brant was astonished by the overpowering sensation of protectiveness that swamped him. Grace Barclay was going to be the mother of the only child he would ever have. Every man wanted to have the very best woman in the world be the mother to his child. It was the Madonna effect working on him; a psychologist would probably tell him he was operating under the survival of the fittest instinct. But as he stared at Grace's eyes closed in peaceful sleep, he knew the very best woman for him was growing his child.

Slowly he walked toward the bed. He took the

edge of the blanket, pulling it carefully over Grace's leg so that she was covered. She didn't move, and Brant could tell by her deep breathing that she was thoroughly worn-out. Of course, he had cut into her sleep last night with his late visit. An urge to caress the tiny freckles sprinkled over her cheek possessed him, but he couldn't risk disturbing her sleep. Instead he went downstairs, kicked off his boots and made himself comfortable on the sofa. Grace looked fine to him now, but just in case, he wanted to be here for her if she needed anything.

You need to think about how our parents' divorce affected you. Cami's voice disturbed his relaxation.

"No, I don't," he said out loud. "I've got everything under control."

GRACE AWAKENED, stretching languorously. The sun no longer streamed in her window as it had when she'd gone to sleep. It was late Sunday afternoon, and she should be making plans for work tomorrow, but the rest had felt too wonderful. She'd needed it, and she knew why. Brant's intrusion in her life had exhausted her emotional state. With any luck, she wouldn't have to face him again—perhaps until the barbecue that was being planned for Cami.

Sighing with refreshed contentment, Grace went into the bathroom that adjoined her room, retrieving a glass of water. Putting it on the nightstand, she raised the window in her room about three inches to let in the soothing spring breeze. Of course, this was the very window Brant had thrown gravel at last night, but she shouldn't have to worry about a repeat episode.

She had made it perfectly clear to him that she

didn't want to see him, except when she had to. They could be civil—for Cami's sake. After the baby was born, they would have to be a little more civil, but, Grace told herself as she sank into bed again, that gave her some time to forgive him for his outrageous, he-man approach to his rights where she was concerned.

BRANT BOLTED UPRIGHT on the sofa, alerted by a squeaking sound from upstairs. Instantly he wondered if Grace was okay. He listened intently, not hearing any further movement. The noise could have been a sound on the street as a car or truck went by, but maybe he should check on Grace again.

Quietly he went back up the stairs, allowing himself a fast peek over the stairwell. Grace was still in bed, though she had turned over, her back to him now. Frowning, he wondered what the noise might have been. Obviously she was still asleep, so she hadn't made the sound. Walking into her room, Brant glanced around, his gaze immediately caught by the barely moving lace hanging from the top of the canopy. The window was open now, and that meant—

"Brant Durning! What in blazes are you doing in my house?" Grace demanded, rolling in a cumbersome fashion as she tried to hoist herself out of the bed.

He backed up quickly, knowing he was in big trouble. She would have discovered his presence eventually, but her bedroom was a bad place to have been caught. "You didn't look well at lunch—"

"Lunch was over four hours ago! Don't tell me you've been in my house all this time! Did you pick one of my locks?"

"Now, Grace," Brant said soothingly. As she made it out of bed, her bare legs caught his attention. The huge T-shirt she wore rode up to the middle of her thighs, and he decided that, if anything, Grace filled out from pregnancy was an even more attractive woman than she'd been before. "I didn't break in. I had Cami—"

"I might have known! Poor Cami! How dare you manipulate her so you could get into my house?" She pointed menacingly toward the stairwell. "Get out, right now."

"Please, Grace, I—"

"I won't listen to anything you have to say, Brant, not while you've concealed yourself under the pretense of being concerned for me. Frankly, you're getting on my nerves."

That hurt his feelings. All he wanted was to get on some kind of caring footing with Grace, and she wouldn't let him. "I'm not trying to, honest. But Grace, you looked so green at lunch I was honestly worried."

"Well, if you're that thin-skinned, you ought to be glad you missed out on the really fun parts of pregnancy." Grace ran a hand through her hair. "Please, just go, Brant. This is my only day to relax. I can't if you're jumping out at me from the shadows."

His gaze dropped instinctively to her belly. It pushed firm and round against the soft-looking T-shirt. "You're making this mighty hard on me, Grace. How can I take care of you if you don't let me?"

Don't want me was what his mind really won-

dered. Brant couldn't imagine not taking care of
Grace. She didn't know how much she needed him.

"Brant, go away. Your protective routine is tire-
some, and way too late."

"That's not my fault, Grace. I would have felt the
same way I do now six months ago if you hadn't
hidden this problem from me."

Her stomach, large and distended, couldn't be hidden by a Mack truck at this point, Grace thought with
great embarrassment. Of course Brant would rush in
with his Sir Galahad ideas when she was at her most
unattractive. "Let's not rehash this," she snapped.
"I have a little time left before I have to allow you
visitation rights."

"Visitation rights?"

She couldn't help noticing the paling beneath his
tanned skin. Instantly Grace felt sorry for her harsh
words. "Brant, all I mean is that I know you're going
to be a good father. Since the minute you found out
you were going to be one, you've been pestering me.
All I'm saying is that there's no baby here now, so
can't you just wait three more months to assert your
fatherly rights?"

"You make it sound like my intentions are solely
for the sake of the baby, Grace. While I definitely
want to care for my child, I also want to take care
of you."

"Fine." Grace told herself to ignore how handsome Brant looked, standing in the hallway with that
pleading look in his blue eyes. Jet-black hair only
emphasized the rugged planes of his face, the determined squareness of his jaw. "Take care of me by
leaving, please. I can't keep fending you off."

He was silent for a moment. "Maybe I don't want you to."

"I'm not going to allow you to waltz casually back into my life as if you never left me," Grace said quietly.

"Do you want me to beg? Romance you? Send flowers?"

She shook her head. "No, Brant. I want none of the above. I want peace and quiet and a chance to enjoy this last part of my pregnancy without you haunting me at every turn. I can't relax with you in Fairhaven. In fact, I almost think it would be better if you took this time to take another cattle buying trip." She dropped her gaze at the hurt in his eyes. "Fortunately I'm leaving tomorrow myself."

Brant's gaze skittered in the direction of Grace's glance. A closed suitcase and an overnight bag sat beside the entrance to her bathroom. His chest tightened at the implication of what she was saying. This time, she was the one leaving. She had family in another state; surely she wouldn't leave him—the same way he'd once left her?

Fear made his words cruel. "Grace, if you're hoping to scare me into a marriage proposal, it isn't going to happen." The stunned widening of her eyes made him wish he hadn't said it.

"Believe me, Brant, the last thing I want is to marry you."

"So where are you going?" He wanted desperately to hear her say she wasn't going to stay away until the baby was born. If that was her plan, he'd have to do something drastic to keep her in Fairhaven. He'd have to do something so drastic he couldn't even wrap his mind around what he knew would be required.

"It's none of your business, but I'll tell you, if you promise to leave once I do," Grace stated. "You're ruining my Sunday relaxation. I'm not above calling Sheriff John to haul you out of here, Brant."

He could tell she meant it. Exasperated, Brant knew she had him with that threat. The last thing he wanted was to bring more attention to their untimely situation. "You won't need to."

"All right. I'm going to New York on a buying trip."

"New York!" His voice contained the same amount of enthusiasm as if she'd said she was going to the other side of the world. "You can't fly in your condition!"

Grace's eyes shot flames. "I already have a good doctor, Brant. I don't need you butting in any more than you have. Now go." She pointed down the stairs.

Brant's insides had turned into a mass of Jell-O. He couldn't believe she meant it. Yet, her bags were packed and waiting. Anything could happen to the stubborn woman in New York! In her advanced state, she would be easy prey for petty thieves. She might go into labor on the airplane. For heaven's sake, she didn't even look as if she'd fit into an airplane lavatory comfortably!

"Grace," he began, but she shook her head.

"Five seconds and I call John. His number is on my speed-dial, by his own request. Go!"

He set his jaw. "I'm going."

"Thank you."

He hesitated on the stair another moment. Grace shook her head again. There wasn't anything else to say. Brant stomped down the stairs, stuffed his feet into the boots he'd shed earlier and was very careful not to let the door slam on his way out.

The lock shot home behind him. He jumped, terribly insulted by the sound. Grace was locking him out of her house and obviously her heart. Didn't the woman understand what torment she was putting him through? Now she was going off all by herself to New York City, when she couldn't even make it through a Sunday lunch at the Yellowjacket without turning pale and frightening him out of a day's worth of deodorant.

There was no help for it. Grace didn't know it yet, but as long as she had his baby in her body, she was stuck with him. It was a package deal.

She wasn't going anywhere without him.

GRACE ALLOWED HERSELF a sigh of relief as she finally ran Brant off. Those five more seconds she'd threatened him with hadn't been because she wanted him to leave as much as she needed him to leave. In all the time she had loved Brant Durning, she had prayed he would return her affection. It was too difficult to sternly turn away the strength of protection he was offering her.

She wandered into the kitchen for a snack. Opening the refrigerator, she found a sack containing the lunch she'd ordered at the Yellowjacket. Tears jumped into her eyes as she sniffled to herself somewhat piteously. Brant was determined to care for her. While that was extremely attractive, she just couldn't allow herself to get used to it. Without the baby,

Brant wouldn't be thinking two thoughts about her, and the knowledge broke Grace's heart.

"Poor little baby," she whispered, stroking a loving hand around her rounded stomach. "Your daddy's a wonderful man. He's going to love you an awful lot."

She hoped the baby would understand the predicament he'd been born into. Two parents, both of whom would love him dearly, but who couldn't give him a family.

Grace lost her appetite. Shoving the food back inside the refrigerator, she hurried back up the stairs. Slamming her window shut so she wouldn't have to worry about Brant deciding to scale her house to check on her through the window, Grace busied herself making a list of things she wanted to look for while she was in New York City. While wedding gowns and accessories were the top priority for the trip, she also intended to look for a baby layette. She was going to enjoy her two days away from Fairhaven—and Brant.

THE NEXT MORNING, Grace settled herself into the airplane seat as best she could. She'd been assigned a middle seat, which annoyed her. She had tried without success to change it, but there had been a last-minute sell-out of seats. She was too darned big to fit comfortably in this tiny little chair, and who knew how many times she'd have to get up to use the bathroom?

Sighing, Grace closed her eyes. She should have checked her seat location when she'd bought the ticket. All she could hope for now was that maybe her aisle seat mate would have mercy on her. After all, it would be better to exchange seats than have to allow her to squeeze by every thirty minutes.

"Excuse me," a deep voice said.

Grace's eyes flew open. "Kyle!"

He handed her a dozen red roses wrapped in cellophane. "Would you believe I just happen to be going to New York City?"

"No, I wouldn't."

"That's my seat over there."

"When did you decide to do this?"

He showed her his boarding pass, so Grace maneuvered into the aisle so he could take the seat by the window. "Last week, when you told me you were planning a buying trip." He sat, moving the seat belt in her chair so she could sit comfortably. "I hope you don't mind, Grace. I just didn't like the idea of you being all alone in New York."

"I've done it before," she said wryly. Though she was touched by his concern, she had really been looking forward to some time to herself on this trip. But what could she say to this man who had offered to marry her? Go away?

"I know you have." Kyle's voice lacked any kind of condescension. "But you haven't gone to New York pregnant."

Grace stiffly held the roses in her lap. What was she going to do with these, anyway? Standing, she reached to put them in the overhead bin on top of her overnight bag. A large male hand closed over hers to help.

"Brant!" she exclaimed, glancing over her shoulder. Her heart started racing like mad. Neither man was going to be pleased to see the other. "What are you doing here?"

"I—" He halted his explanation, his gaze narrowing on Kyle. "I see I'm not necessary."

The last thing she wanted was for Brant to think she had planned a trip with Kyle. Grace's mind emptied of any possible explanation for Kyle's presence. The baby kicked inside her, and suddenly Grace felt a bit nauseated.

"Listen, both of you—"

"Good afternoon, and welcome to Flight 1211, bound for New York City," the flight attendant announced over the microphone.

Grace hadn't made it through lunch yesterday sitting between these two males. There was no way she could endure a long flight sandwiched between them.

"Please, I beg both of you to deplane." Pushing Brant aside in the aisle, much to the annoyance of passengers who wanted to get around them, Grace stood so that Kyle could get out. "I know you both have the best intentions, and I'm truly touched in an astonished sort of way, but it's just too much. Please."

Kyle and Brant eyed each other with hostility, neither moving. "Please," Grace said softly. "Both of you go now. I will call each of you when I return, I promise, but you're both making me crazy."

"I don't see why I should have to," Kyle stated reasonably. "After all, I've asked you to marry me. Brant is the one without a good reason for being here."

"Don't tell me I don't have a good reason for being here!" Brant roared. "And what do you mean, you asked Grace to marry you?"

Interested onlookers peered over the seat in front

and back of them, while others had stopped in the aisle, watching the unfolding drama with interest.

The pilot needs to flip on the air-conditioning, Grace thought irrationally. She felt faint, and mortified.

"Is there a problem?" a flight attendant asked impatiently.

"Yes, there is," Grace said. "These two men are bothering me. I insist you change my seat at once. Let them sit together, since they so badly want to."

"Aw, lady, give them a break," a balding man said. "It's obvious you liked one of 'em," he said, with a pointed glance at her stomach.

Grace ripped the seat ticket from the man's fingers. "Thank you, sir, for offering to exchange seats with me. Help yourself."

"Wait, Grace," Kyle said, getting to his feet. "I don't want you to be angry with me. I'll get off the plane, if you promise to call me at once when you get to the hotel so I'll know you've arrived safely."

"Thank you," Grace said on a sigh of relief.

She waited while Kyle made his way into the aisle. "Thank you for the roses," she said, pressing a kiss to his cheek. "I will call you soon."

He looked vaguely uncomfortable. "I'm not going unless he goes, too." It was clear Kyle was waiting for Brant to be as chivalrous as he was.

"Oh, for heaven's sake!" She felt pushed to the limit of her endurance. "I thought at least you, Kyle, were going to be reasonable."

"I'm trying to be, Grace, but he's no gentleman. I don't trust Brant as far as I can throw him."

"Why, you—" Brant reached over Grace's head to make a grab for Kyle's collar.

"Please!" Grace pushed Brant away, accidentally sending Kyle against the balding man.

"Lady, if I'm gonna take your seat, I don't want to be a party to fisticuffs," he complained. "I like to sleep on plane flights."

"Mind your own business!" she admonished him. Taking a deep breath, she was just about to grab her bags and leave the plane when Brant's deep voice halted her.

"All right, I'll go." He stared menacingly at Kyle. "But I'm out the price of a plane ticket. Don't expect me to bring any more of my animal practice your way."

Brant stalked past everyone in the aisle, glaring at Kyle as he went by.

"Fine! Expect me to boycott beef!" Kyle stuck out his chest, but Brant only shoved his cowboy hat down farther on his head and slunk off toward the exit.

Grace sighed in exasperation. "Thank heavens! Now, if you'll just—"

"I'm going, I'm going," Kyle said, his tone rueful.

"Good! I can get my seat back," the balding man exclaimed, snatching his boarding pass from Grace's hand. He lurched down the aisle toward the back of the plane.

"I appreciate it, Kyle. Thank you for being a good sport."

He touched her cheek softly. "Say yes when you come back, Grace."

Kyle turned around and walked away. Grace was so relieved she didn't know what to do.

''Quit staring,'' she said to everyone watching her. ''The show's over.''

Sliding into her seat, she realized with relief that the two seats on either side of her would now be free. She wouldn't have to worry about being cramped during the flight. ''Ahh,'' she sighed, allowing herself to unwind in the space now afforded her by the exit of the men in her life.

What was she going to do about them? she wondered. On the one hand, she had to seriously consider Kyle's marriage proposal and the emotional security a whole family would mean for her baby. On the other hand, Brant was likely to be such an impediment to the happiness of any married life she tried to enjoy that she seriously doubted the wisdom of accepting Kyle's proposal.

Besides which, Brant owns my heart. Therein lay the biggest problem of all. The stubborn man was so bullheaded that he would do anything for her, except become her husband. He was determined to retain his protective intrusion into her life without the benefit of a marriage certificate.

Well, she would fix that with him as soon as she returned from New York City. With time, perhaps Brant's novelty with being a father would wear thin, but she couldn't count on that. She would just tell him, in no uncertain terms, and more firmly even than she had told him at her house, that he was not welcome to make himself at home in her life anymore. He was thoroughly disrupting it.

The flight attendant instructed the passengers to prepare for takeoff. The plane began taxiing down the runway. Grace closed her eyes, feeling her spirits lift even as the plane began gathering speed, lifting into a diagonal ascent.

Whoosh! She suddenly felt someone land in the seat next to her. Grace started, her eyes flying open to see Brant buckling the seat belt. Her mouth dropped open as everyone seated around them started clapping.

Chapter Five

"What are you doing, Brant?" she snapped.

"Just act like I'm not here," he told her, his blue eyes alight with mischief.

"You were supposed to get off the plane!" She was furious with his deception.

"Aw, babe, say you're glad to see me."

Grace glared up over the seats, and the clapping subsided. "Guess we know now which one's the father!" the balding man called from the back of the plane.

"I had my money on the cowboy," an elderly woman said. "He looks like he knows how to get out of the chute."

"Honestly!" Grace wouldn't dignify that with a response. She lowered herself into the seat. "The last thing I am is glad to see you, Brant. How dare you deceive poor Kyle like that?"

"Wasn't very gentlemanly of me," he admitted. "'Course, he's not very intelligent if he expects you to carry a dozen roses all the way to New York."

She could tell by the devilish delight in his eyes that he didn't care at all about Kyle. "I suppose you expect me to be more impressed by your John Wayne sling-the-girl-over-the-saddle routine.''

His eyes softened as he leaned his head against the seat. He patted her hand, then grabbed a magazine from the seat pocket in front of him. ''How long is this flight, anyway? Four, five hours? Long enough for me to convince you of my earnest regret for deceiving Kyle, and for slinging you over my saddle.''

He was laughing at her! Grace was so outraged she couldn't speak for a moment. ''I'm going to sleep. Do not speak to me the entire time this plane is in the air, or I will be tempted to scream until they move you to another seat.''

''Plane's full.'' His tone told her he still thought he was going to worm out of her wrath.

''I'll switch seats with the bald man,'' she threatened.

''Okay.'' He held up his hands. ''I promise not to say a word the entire time the plane is in the air.''

''Thank you.'' She put the armrest of the seat next to the window up, allotting herself the breadth of both chairs. Scooching over to the window, she snatched a pillow from a passing flight attendant, and made herself as comfortable as possible. When the seat belt light turned off, she removed her shoes and curled her legs up into the seat next to her. This way she was almost comfortable, and might sleep the entire way to New York. It would be wonderful relief from being reminded of Brant's presence in the seat next to her feet.

Almost as if he sensed her thoughts, Brant absently reached over, never taking his eyes from the magazine, and began rubbing her feet. Grace rolled her eyes, sighing. He would keep his word by not speaking, but he would assault her senses in other ways. The massaging motion of Brant's strong fingers felt heavenly to her sore, swollen feet. Surrendering for the moment, Grace closed her eyes and willed herself to sleep.

AT THE HOTEL a few hours later, Grace eyed the hotel clerk with disbelief. "What do you mean, I don't have a reservation? I have a confirmation number. I reserved a room over a month ago."

"I'm sorry." He made another run through his computer. "Some error was obviously made. Did you call the 1-800 number or this hotel specifically?"

"I made reservations using the 1-800 number, of course," Grace said through clenched teeth. "There wasn't any reason to pay for the call, and I've never had any trouble getting a room in this hotel for any of my business trips before." She was careful to emphasize trips in the plural so the clerk would know her future patronage was in jeopardy if he didn't locate a room for her pronto. It was frustrating that this situation had to develop with Brant looking over her shoulder. She could take care of this matter; she did not need him tagging along to take care of her, as he seemed to think.

"I'm terribly sorry, ma'am. Let me get the manager for you."

"Is there another problem?"

"Well, actually, yes." He looked terribly embarrassed. "There's a large convention in town—"

"And you're booked." Grace couldn't believe it.

"Yes. I think that's why I'm not showing anything with your reservation number on it. There must have been a computer glitch of some kind." His eyes briefly skimmed her stomach in a sympathetic way. "Please wait right here. Perhaps the manager can arrange for you to have a room at another hotel."

"I don't want to stay in another hotel! My appointments aren't far from here. This is convenient for me."

Brant stepped up beside her. "Check my reservation for me, please. Brant Durning."

The desk clerk quickly checked his computer. "Yes," he said with a sigh of relief. "I do show a room for you, sir."

"Give it to her," Brant said briskly. "I can find another hotel to stay in."

"Are you sure?" Grace hadn't counted on him coming to her rescue in this way. "You don't mind going somewhere else?"

"No, I don't. If there's no room at the inn, then there's no room. I don't want you traipsing around town trying to find a bed." His eyes roamed over her, concerned. "I'll get a bellcap to take your suitcase and overnight bag up."

"I'm terribly sorry for the inconvenience," the desk clerk offered. "In the future, please—"

Brant waved him off. Grace stared as Brant went to retrieve her bags. She finished checking in, while Brant stood stoically to the side. His eyes narrowed as she approached. "I appreciate you giving up your room."

"Never mind. Do you have everything else you need?"

"I do." She hesitated for a moment, telling herself it served him right not to have a room. He shouldn't have followed her to New York in the first place!

Yet, she would still be out a room. "Brant, the room has double beds."

"I'll ask for a king-size bed if you'd be more comfortable."

"No!" She dropped her gaze. "I was going to say that I'll be out most of tomorrow. The room will be empty. It doesn't make much sense for you to have to find a room in another hotel when I won't be around anyway."

"Are you inviting me to bunk with you?"

She couldn't raise her eyes to meet his. "In a totally platonic way, yes, I am. If you understand that..."

Her voice trailed off. She wasn't sure how to say exactly what she wanted him to understand.

"If I understand that I get the bed by the window, and you get the bed nearest the bathroom."

"Exactly," she breathed out on a sigh of relief.

"Ah." He considered her words. "It's okay, Grace. I didn't come to New York to make love to you, though that would be nice. I came to spend time with you. I can do that from a bed three feet away from yours."

"Thanks for understanding, Brant." She was glad he understood she didn't want to be pushed into any new layer of their relationship. She just wasn't ready.

"Come on," he said, taking her arm. "Let's get these bags upstairs. If you'll allow me to, I'll buy you dinner in the hotel restaurant."

She hesitated for the slightest second.

"Don't worry, Grace. I know what the playing rules are. It'll be dinner, and nothing else."

"Okay," she said ungraciously, not certain how much time the two of them could spend together before things might turn accidentally and disastrously romantic. "Dinner, and nothing else."

THIRTY MINUTES LATER, Grace sat at a dinner table that was covered by a white tablecloth adorned by a glowing candle. It might be romantic, if her dinner companion wasn't Brant.

"Now that we're in New York, I want you to explain what Kyle meant when he said he'd asked you to marry him." Brant's eyebrows were thunderclouds of disapproval.

Grace shook her head. "Don't glower at me."

"When were you going to tell me?"

"What difference can it possibly make, Brant? You and I have resolved our situation to our mutual satisfaction. We are free to lead our separate lives outside of the baby."

"You are *not* free to marry Kyle Macaffee!" Brant's eyes revealed his contempt. "Grace, you're talking crazy."

She lost her appetite, though the food was wonderful and she'd skipped the airplane lunch. "I'm exhausted, Brant. I'm going up to the room, if you'll excuse me."

She got up and walked out of the restaurant. Never in her life had she ever done such a thing, but Brant's chauvinistic attitude was wearing her down. For her sake, and the baby's, she needed a stress-free environment. Being with Brant was more stressful than having a bride panic at the last minute that her dress wasn't quite right!

The hotel room was at least quiet, Grace thought with a sigh of relief. She went inside and closed the door, enjoying the silence and the peach and green decor. Getting out of her maternity outfit, she had a quick shower, making certain the bathroom door was locked securely. When she finished bathing, she peeped cautiously around the door, but Brant still hadn't returned. With a sigh of relief, Grace slipped on a huge T-shirt, crawled into bed and promptly fell asleep.

BRANT SAT AT THE TABLE trying to finish his meal after Grace left, but he was fighting a losing battle. He didn't have any desire to eat. The revelation that Macaffee had the nerve to propose to the mother of Brant's child had kept him simmering all afternoon. He'd waited for the best time to ask Grace about it. Apparently he hadn't picked the right time—but the time was never going to be right where Macaffee was concerned.

He threw the dinner roll he was eating back onto the plate. Grace couldn't possibly be considering the veterinarian's proposal! Didn't she know how that would make him, Brant, look? As if he wasn't man enough to take care of his own offspring!

Would I propose to a woman who was carrying someone else's child?

Not likely. He wouldn't even propose to the one who was carrying *his* child. And he loved Grace.

Brant bowed his head. Why couldn't she be satisfied with that? Didn't she know that the best of marriages didn't last forever? That marriage wasn't a guarantee there wouldn't be heartbreak down the road in twenty, thirty years?

A memory of his parents splitting up tried to edge into his mind, but Brant shoved it away. How could he convince Grace to see his point in this matter?

What he was offering her was honest; it was from the heart. If he had to change his feelings to suit her, in the end, their relationship wouldn't be what either of them wanted.

Grace Barclay Macaffee, his errant brain reminded him. The obstinate woman might actually marry that veterinarian, just to spite Brant! Women in town were crazy over Kyle. Privately Brant knew Kyle was a good, fair man. He'd been throwing business Kyle's way almost exclusively since the man opened his practice. Kyle had a way with sick, injured things; many a case Brant had thought was going to end with a shotgun or a hypodermic had turned around nicely under Kyle's capable hands.

Damn it, Brant thought angrily as he signed the dinner tab. *This is one case Kyle Macaffee isn't going to be doing any doctorin' on.* He caught the elevator, striding to the hotel room he and Grace were occupying, fully prepared to have it out with her over this matter.

In one of the beds she lay, soundly and deeply asleep. All the righteous anger left Brant immediately. He looked at her, securely tucked under the covers, even to her chin. She had the air-conditioning unit in the room going full-blast, cold enough to chill Alaska. She appeared obliviously comfortable.

There was no help for it. He'd need an igloo to survive in this room tonight. Stripping off his clothes, he took a fast shower. Then he crawled into bed, careful not to disturb Grace, and molded himself against her back.

SOMEHOW, Grace wasn't surprised when she awakened to discover Brant wrapped around her as if he were a warm, furry bear. He hadn't played fair ever since he decided to weasel his way onto the airplane. Painful memories of how much she enjoyed snuggling with him assaulted her, so Grace got up and went into the bathroom to get dressed and put on her makeup. If she was very quiet, perhaps Brant wouldn't notice her leaving. It would be nice to start her day without having a verbal sparring match with him.

When she emerged from the bathroom, she found a bright-eyed Brant staring at her appreciatively, already dressed.

"Breakfast is over there." He pointed to a tray that had been delivered while she was in the bathroom.

Her stomach bottomed out. "I'm not hungry."

"There's orange juice and apple juice," he said, ignoring her comment, "and some breakfast stuff like cereal and bagels. I didn't know which was healthier to eat when a woman is expecting."

"Brant Durning," Grace said, putting her hands on her hips, "you listen to me, and listen good. I did just fine without you before. I very much resent you trying to take over my life." She turned to go, and opened the door.

He shot up from the bed, putting a hand just above her head to keep the door closed. "Wait a minute, Grace. I kinda thought I was being considerate. I thought you might prefer having something to eat first thing. Isn't that supposed to help morning sickness?"

"That passed in the first trimester," she said between clenched teeth. It was extremely difficult to ignore the pickup in her heart rate. If only the man wasn't so darned sexy!

"Oh."

To his credit, he did appear embarrassed by her reference to the morning sickness she had endured. Grace drew a deep breath, willing herself to sound more patient. "Please move, Brant. I have an early morning meeting with a vendor."

"Well, hang on a sec. I'll just follow along, you know, walk you there. Can't be too careful in New York."

"Brant, I'm going alone. I'll be fine."

He didn't pay any attention, heading into the bathroom to run a comb through his hair and quickly brush his teeth. "Just let me walk you," he said around a mouthful of toothpaste.

Suddenly Grace knew how she could keep Brant from accompanying her. "You know, I just don't think you'll enjoy hanging around all day escorting me from place to place. I've got appointments in the market, then I'm planning to attend a show."

"A show? Hey, I'd love to take in a show with you. Hang on just another sec."

Slyly Grace said, "It's a wedding gown fashion show."

He stiffened, blowing mouthwash into the sink.

The discomfort on his face made Grace laugh. Of all the things in the world Brant wouldn't want to be faced with, it was wedding gowns. She decided to jab the needle in a little deeper. "Not very interesting to a man, I know. And my day only gets less exciting. After the show, I've made an appointment with a friend of mine to look at some of her baby layette samples."

"Okay." Brant brightened, immediately leaving the bathroom to retrieve his wallet. "I don't know what a baby layette is, but I'm game to learn."

She couldn't believe it. "Brant, baby layette is just a term for baby stuff! You don't want to pick out towels, clothes, washcloths—"

"Hey, little man, shopping for your first clothes in New York City." He grinned hugely and reached out to pat Grace's tummy. The grin disappeared from his face the second his hand made contact. His gaze held Grace's, a mixture of puzzlement and astonishment widening his eyes. "I didn't know that was how it felt," he said hoarsely.

Grace's blood thundered in her ears. After a second, Brant's palm spread slightly, exploring. The baby chose that moment to stick out an elbow or heel.

"Grace!" Brant yelped. His eyes got even wider at the movement under his hand. "It's alive!"

Grace laughed at his amazement. "Haven't you felt Cami's stomach?"

Shock jerked his hand away from the amazing feel of her stomach. "Why would I want to do that?"

"You're going to be an uncle, Brant, whether you like the idea or not. I just thought maybe you'd, I don't know, hugged your sister when you got back into town, at least..." Her words dwindled off.

Brant backed up a step, temporarily confused by what Grace was suggesting. Hug Cami? Heck, no, he'd been more disposed to give her a good solid whumping. "I...I didn't think about it," he said lamely. He eyed Grace's stomach again with some trepidation. "She's not as big as you are, and I guess it never occurred to me..."

"You were gone for three months and didn't hug your sister when you returned?"

He didn't like the accusatory expression on Grace's face. "If you're going to make your appointment, we'd better get going," he said abruptly. "Do you want any of this juice or not? I think my son ought to at least have a healthy snack before he starts his day."

It was diversionary tactics, and Grace was never fooled by those, but at least she walked over and took a glass of orange juice from the tray. He was relieved when she grabbed a muffin as well.

"I'll eat this on the way," she said, swishing past him.

Her perfume teased him as she swept by, her hair all gold and shiny as it fell in long, attractive curls over the top of her navy blouse.

"Fine." He closed the door behind them. "Let's go get some baby lingerie."

"Layette!" Grace called over her shoulder.

"Layette," he repeated, trying the new word on his tongue. Grace's disapproval hurt his feelings, because, deep inside, he knew she was right about his sister. Maybe if he got the hang of this baby layette stuff, he'd pick up an extra one for Cami as a peace offering.

Dang, but it had never occurred to him that, not only was he going to be a father, he was going to be an uncle as well.

IT WAS ANNOYING that Brant had to remember while Grace was inside the market that he had not fully gotten it through her head that she was not marrying Macaffee. Brant pushed away from the wall he was leaning against, shooting an impatient look at his watch. She was taking too long!

What if she's picking something out for herself?

He felt ill. Grace would love to wear a gown like she'd been fitting other women into all these years. Like any woman, she must dream of being a bride. Macaffee was offering to make that dream come true. Brant was offering her security, which she didn't seem too impressed by, and he was offering her his steadfast companionship, but that didn't seem to be enough, either.

That baby was *his*. The woman was his, too, though she was acting as if she didn't know it. His son wasn't going to ride on a tractor with anybody but his own father. A grin spread over his face just thinking about holding a little boy-body between his legs as he steered a tractor over the family acreage. He would point out places he'd loved to explore as a child—

Feminine giggles jolted him out of his reverie. Two young women, probably early twenties, were staring at him.

"You look like the Marlboro man without a mustache," one of them said.

They were kind of cute. Brant puffed up a little under their admiration. "I don't smoke, though. Smoking's bad for your health," he told them.

"He talks just like a real cowboy!" the other one cried with delight. "Can we have our picture taken with you?"

Only in New York, Brant thought, would anyone think his cowboy hat and boots were a fashion statement. "Sure," he said easily.

One girl ran to stand beside him, while the other

snapped a picture with her camera. They quickly traded places, and Brant smiled obligingly for the last shot.

"What is going *on?*"

Grace's astounded voice let the air out of Brant's pride. "Just playing tourist," he said.

"You certainly are." She looked angrier than he'd ever seen her. Grace looked...hurt. Brant realized he had made an error the size of the Empire State Building and knew it was time to go into damage control.

The two girls stared at Grace bravely because Brant had allowed them to take his picture. "Would you mind taking a picture so both of us can be in it with him?"

Before Brant could head off what he knew must be coming, Grace had dropped the package she'd been carrying and thrust the full width of her belly next to Brant. "I'll be happy to, if you don't mind taking one of all *three* of us with my camera," she said too sweetly.

The girls' jaws dropped. "Um, we um—"

Grace smiled, catlike. "I understand."

"We've gotta catch a bus. 'Bye!" they called, hurriedly strolling away.

"Grace, I—"

"Don't say a word, Brant. I'm surprised, but not shocked."

Grace picked up her package, turning on her heel to hurry off. Brant had to lengthen his stride to keep up. "It was harmless, Grace. They were just girls, for heaven's sake!"

"And you just couldn't resist playing big, strong, cowboy." She didn't slow down.

He reached over to take her package from her. "I'm not sure why you're so upset, babe."

"Upset! Upset!" Grace halted, whirling to face him. "Who's upset?"

Brant watched her warily. "I think you are."

"Well, why would I be upset? Because while I'm inside working, you're outside playing urban cowboy for a couple of girls who are young enough to leave their bras at home?"

He hadn't given any consideration to their breasts. "Ah—"

"I mean, I know you were probably impressed by the fact that their bottoms were still so tight they could sit on a crack on this pavement and make perfectly perpendicular lines, but damn it—"

To Brant's utter disbelief, Grace burst into tears. "Hey, babe. Don't cry." He lowered the package to the concrete and wrapped his arms around her. "I'm sorry. I didn't mean to upset you."

She sniffled against his chest. He kind of liked holding her against him, feeling her need him, though he wanted her to quit crying.

"Is it a hormone thing?" he asked, looking for a reasonable explanation for Grace's distress. It just wasn't like her to fly off the handle.

"No, it's because you're a jackass." She kept her face hidden against him. "I'm all pushed out of shape, Brant! I'm like a straw with a watermelon inside it. My ankles are the size of your biceps, and you're letting two beautiful girls paw you. How am I supposed to feel?"

Ah. What she was feeling was suddenly clear to him. "You're just a little jealous, honey, but—"

She jerked away from him and went speeding

down the sidewalk. "Grace, wait!" He snatched up the package and took after her. "What did I say?"

"You bigheaded baboon," she flung at him. "Naturally your preoccupation with yourself won't allow you to think of anything but how I must be eaten up with jealousy over you. You're just so wonderful, I'm not certain we can both fit inside this taxi."

She hailed the one closest to the curb and hopped in, giving directions to the driver. Brant barely had time to close the door before the taxi zoomed away.

"What am I missing here, babe?"

"Your ego? You must have left it on the sidewalk since we're both occupying the same seat."

Her eyes were large with sarcastic innocence. Brant wasn't sure how to deal with this fiery Grace.

"Please tell me, because I can't make it right if I don't know what I'm doing wrong." He hoped she would see how much he really wanted to make her happy.

She took her gaze from his and stared out the opposite window. "I feel unattractive."

His mouth fell open. She had never been more beautiful in her entire life! "Like you couldn't sit on a crack and line up perpendicularly?" he asked carefully.

"Exactly."

He shook his head, reaching over to sweep her into his lap. "I'm sorry. I shouldn't have been playing tourist with two babes."

"Brant!"

He laughed, nuzzling her neck. "Grace, you're beautiful. Maybe I should have told you sooner, but I've always been attracted to you."

"I know *that*." Her freckles stood out a little with

a rush of color to her skin. "I wouldn't be in this condition otherwise." She sighed. "I just didn't enjoy having to fight off the cover girls from hell."

"Grace." He pressed a kiss against her temple. "I—"

"Hey!" the taxi driver called. "No neckin' in my cab!"

She slid off Brant's lap. "I'm paying you to watch the road, sir." To Brant, she said, "I'm sorry I went hysterical. You were right. It probably was only hormonal imbalance." She looked away, obviously saving face.

"That's okay." Secretly Brant was a little amused, and maybe a little pleased that Grace still thought enough of him to let her hormones go awry. "Now where to?"

"My final appointment, then I'm finished for the day."

"Baby stuff?" Brant sat straighter, his attention caught. "So what's in this big box we've been lugging around?"

Grace didn't look his way. "A wedding gown."

Chapter Six

Brant recoiled as if he were holding a boxed cobra. "Wedding gown?"

"Uh-huh."

Surely she hadn't picked out a dress for herself. Surely she wasn't giving consideration to Macaffee's proposal. "Can I ask why?" he demanded. Fear gave his voice a jealous, sharp edge.

"It really wouldn't be of interest to you, Brant. I'll hold the box if it's a problem." She looked out at the passing scenery, without giving him so much as a blink at her expression.

"No, I don't mind carrying it." He desperately wanted to know what its presence in the taxi meant.

The cab pulled to the curb. Grace paid the driver before Brant even realized they were at their destination. He wedged himself out the door with the large box, and saw Grace heading toward the glass doors of a building at a good clip. Obviously she was still out of sorts with him. Brant didn't think he could blame her, actually. He shouldn't have let those girls take his picture, but it wouldn't happen again.

Grace held the door open, and Brant squeezed past her, then tried to keep pace as she headed toward a door with no name on the outside. Once past the door, however, he could see hangers with all kinds of little baby things hanging from rolling racks and on the wall. "Wow," he said.

"These are lines of kids' clothing my friend is taking orders for. Usually she only works with department stores and boutiques, but she told me to come over and look at her samples."

A woman taller than Grace came out of the back of the showroom. "Grace! You made it."

The two women hugged. "I did, and I brought you something, Jana. First, let me introduce you to..." She hesitated, obviously not having considered how she would introduce Brant. "This is my friend, Brant Durning," she said slowly, "Brant, this is my friend, Jana Watkins."

"You must be a closer friend than me," Jana said with a meaningful smile at Grace's belly. "It's nice to meet you, Brant." He couldn't shake hands very well because of the package he held.

"Jana, here's something I think you'll want to see." Grace took the box from Brant's hands, completely avoiding eye contact with him.

Jana led them from the reception area into an office and put the box on a desk. "Oh!" she exclaimed, pulling the lid off, "It's beautiful, Grace! Absolutely beautiful!"

Jana held the gown against herself. The long slender style suited Jana's height, though Brant instinctively knew that nothing like that would fit on Grace in her condition. He wondered if there was such a thing as maternity bridal wear.

"Do you really like it?" Grace asked, watching

anxiously as Jana hurried to examine her image in a mirror.

"I love it! I knew I could trust you to choose the perfect gown." She hurried over to hug Grace enthusiastically.

Brant's skin grew hot along his collar with embarrassment. Jana obviously knew he was the father of the child Grace was carrying. She had to wonder why Brant wasn't ponying up for a few yards of satin and lace for his woman.

"Thank you." Jana smiled luminously. "My fiancé is going to love you for picking this out. And you for carrying it all the way over here so I could see it, Brant." She smiled so widely, Brant forced a grim smile in return. "Now, come on, you two, and see if I've got anything you'd be interested in."

"I really appreciate this, Jana," Grace said, walking ahead with her friend. Brant followed along at a more calculatedly casual pace. This was women's business. He should have stayed outside on the sidewalk.

No. He'd gotten into more trouble when he'd tried to stay out of the way. Brant crammed his hands into his pockets, trying not to be too interested in the baby garments hanging here and there.

"What about this, Brant?" Jana called merrily.

She held up a bib that read Daddy Did It. It had lace all around its edges, and Brant's neck felt even hotter.

"I don't think it's quite what he had in mind, Jana."

"Well, that was just for starters. Let me show you some coming home outfits that are to die for."

Coming home outfits? Brant pondered that. Didn't

babies just stay at home most of the time, anyway? Why did they need special outfits to come home in?

"Oh, this one's adorable," Grace murmured.

Brant eased over to see what she was admiring. It was the tiniest thing he'd ever seen: white, with a little satin giraffe on the chest area, and little snaps down the front.

"Isn't it sweet?" Grace asked him.

"I—yeah," Brant agreed. "Don't boys wear blue? And isn't that awfully small? I don't want him to be, you know, bound up."

Grace and Jana laughed. "It's a nine-month size, Brant," Jana explained.

"Yeah, well Grace is six months now. She'll be nine months when she delivers, I'm sure. You better get a larger size, Grace."

The women laughed again. Grace shook her head. "I'll take this one in the newborn size, if you've got it, Jana. It's too cute."

They spent an hour looking at outfits and washcloths and stuff Brant had never considered a baby might need. He watched the pile of Grace's selections grow with contentment, until she held up a lace and white dress.

"It's so beautiful! I've never seen anything like it."

Grace's gaze went up and down the dress as if she was looking at heaven. It was tiny, in Brant's eyes, and all that lace was an inexcusable mistake to put on anyone's baby. Any baby worth its salt would be irritated by the itching. He started when she put it in the pile.

"Hey! You're not putting a dress on my son!" he roared at once.

"It's a christening gown," Jana told him.

"I don't care what it is, it's not going home with us. My boy's wearing pants, as is meant to be."

"What's that supposed to mean?" Grace was bridling.

"I really don't know." Brant threw himself into the nearest chair in a huff. "Look, Grace, I'm all for women's lib and everything, but I'm not comfortable with my boy wearing skirts."

"Put the dress back, Jana," Grace said softly. "Brant's done pretty well getting up to speed so far. It'll take a little longer to explain some other things to him."

"Danged right," he muttered. "Hey!" He straightened, his attention caught by an outfit hanging on a display near the wall. "Now that's more what I had in mind."

It was blue jean material anyone could find in any state, connected by snaps to a red handkerchief print shirt he could have bought in Texas, but the outfit came with the requisite snaps down the legs. Brant was delighted he'd found something he could relate to. "I'll take that. Got any boots to go with it?"

"No." Jana laughed, and got the little Western outfit down. "For the first few months, maybe a pair of white bootie socks will suffice."

Brant was disappointed. "Okay. Do you have another one of those Western outfits, then?"

"Brant, I hardly think I'll need two." Grace's eyebrows rose. "I mean, I've probably got enough for one trip, don't you think?"

"The second outfit's for Cami," he said gruffly, not looking at Grace. To Jana, he said, "I'll take a few bibs and washcloths, too, please, none that say anything about daddy doing it.''

He felt Grace lightly touch his arm in approval, which Brant liked, but was careful not to acknowledge. His eyes caught on the white baby gown Grace had so admired. It *was* awfully pretty, but he was going to have to keep a close eye on her and make sure she didn't truss his son up like a mama's boy. Shoot, none of the neighboring rancher's kids would play with his child! ''Jeez. How's he gonna look in Future Farmers of America with a dress on?'' Brant grumbled.

Grace and Jana laughed, dismissing his complaint. Brant tried to grin, as if he'd meant the question to be funny, but he was serious about his boy not wearing that dress.

Christening gown or whatever, that dress looked suspiciously like a wedding gown.

ONE HOUR LATER, they had finished up and returned to the hotel. Grace said her back was hurting, so she went to take a shower. Brant threw himself on the bed and turned on CNN, but his thoughts weren't on the bickering broadcasters.

His thoughts were on what Grace looked like nude. He didn't have the right to know, of course, but his body responded just thinking about it. She'd gotten terribly upset over his antics with the female tourists, but it had never crossed his mind that she might be. Grace put those young things to shame.

Had he ever told her how beautiful he thought she was? During the months they'd gone out as a couple, he couldn't remember saying such to her. Something told him he hadn't—of course he hadn't. Romance wasn't his strong suit.

His gaze slid once again to Kyle's roses, now wilting in the ice bucket Grace had commandeered as a vase. What a dumb thing to do, anyway. If that was romance, Kyle Macaffee had thrown fifty dollars down the drain.

The shower quit, and Grace came out a moment later wearing a flowing caftan. "You look comfortable," he murmured, thinking she also looked gorgeous.

"Oh, I am." She sank onto the opposite bed with a pleased moan. "I'm sorry I can't accommodate you for dinner, Brant."

"It's fine. I'm a bit worn-out myself." Actually he'd been amazed by how much Grace could get done in a day. He wondered if she was pushing it by being so active. "We can order in something from room service."

"That sounds wonderful."

"Do you want me to toss those flowers so I can get you some ice and a soda?"

Grace turned to stare at him. "Toss my flowers? Why would I want you to do that?"

"Well, they're wilting," Brant said pointedly, trying to sound practical. Even he could hear the sheepish sound in his voice. "I didn't think you'd want them anymore."

"They're beautiful! Of course I don't want you to throw them out." Grace sat up.

Brant was tired of looking at the silly things. He supposed Grace would want to tote them back on the plane all the way back to the Dallas airport. "Are you planning on taking them back with you?"

"No."

"Then we can throw them away just a few hours early and be able to use the ice bucket."

"Kyle was sweet to buy those for me!"

"I'd say he was lacking good sense to spend that much money on something that's going in the trash."

"Oh, for heaven's sake, Brant! You wouldn't know romance if it was staring you in the face!"

He halted in the act of reaching for a room service menu. "Grace, if that's what you're looking for, I'm not going to be able to give it to you."

"I didn't ask you to," she said stiffly. "Just don't begrudge it to me if someone else does."

"Fair enough." He slapped the menu back onto the table between their beds and stared at the ceiling. *Mother left Daddy because she'd found a man who would treat her the way she deserved to be treated,* Cami's relentless voice reminded him. Two years after their parents had split up, while Brant was still wrestling with why it had happened, Cami had stated the reason for him in practical terms he had never accepted. Women didn't leave a good home with a solid roof and three square meals, and all the money she could spend on dresses, all for a romantic fling. It just didn't make sense to him.

That reminded him of another no-two-ways-about-it fact. He had to tell his parents that he was going to be a father. Cami had told them of her own predicament, of course, with all the joy and enthusiasm she had for discovering she was going to be a mother.

"Have you told your parents?" he asked with a sidelong glance at Grace.

"Yes." She didn't look at him.

"What did they say?"

"What could they?"

Her coyness wasn't helping him out. Suddenly he knew he didn't want the Barclays to think ill of him for not marrying their daughter. "Do they know the child is mine?"

"Until a few days ago, this child was only mine," Grace said stiffly. "But yes, they know you're the father, Brant."

"What did they say?"

She rolled her head to look at him. "That they were sure you'd do the right thing by me. They've always liked you." She sighed as if she didn't understand why they would.

Brant's collar felt a bit tight. He jerked one of the top buttons open on his shirt and tried to relax. In his own way, he was doing the very best by Grace that he could. Certainly his way wasn't the conventional way, but it was all he could offer.

"What about your folks? Do they know?"

"Not yet. I'll have to tell them soon."

They were silent for a moment. "Maybe you should wait until after Cami's wedding. Two pregnancies in the family out of wedlock might come as a shock to them."

Her voice held a tinge of amusement, but Brant saw nothing funny about any of it. "Don't you think they'll figure it out for themselves when they see you at the wedding, Grace?"

"Well, my maid of honor dress won't lie, that's true."

He closed his eyes, feeling an ominous tightening around the front of his skull.

"Kyle has offered to be my escort to the wedding. Maybe your parents will think—"

"Grace Barclay!" Brant was outraged. "Just pick out what you want me to order you for supper, okay?" The tightening was increasing to an intense viselike feeling. "I'm going to take some aspirin."

He got up to get one when Grace suddenly jumped. "Oh, my!" she exclaimed, rubbing her stomach. Her expression was somewhat pained.

"What is it?"

"I think…he kicked me. Not very gentlemanly of him, was it?" She tried to smile, but her eyes looked tired.

"Can I help?"

She shook her head. "It was probably just a stray—oh!"

"What?" Brant felt helpless.

"Nothing. Go get your aspirin. The little guy is probably in the mood for a little exercise."

"I don't know." Brant wondered how a baby could exercise all cooped up in there. Maybe Grace had pulled a muscle with all her running around today. "Let me look."

"No!" Grace's brows furrowed.

"Oh, come on, Grace. It's nothing I haven't seen before."

"Trust me. You haven't seen this. And you're not going to." She rolled onto her side, keeping her hand firmly on her abdomen, groaning slightly.

"Either you let me look under that thing you're wearing, or I call a doctor." Brant was adamant on this point.

"You're overreacting. It's probably gas."

"Let me look." He reached out and rolled her gently onto her back.

"Gas isn't visible to the naked eye, so there's no reason for you to look."

He reached for the telephone.

"Oh, Brant! For pity's sake. Let me pull a blanket up, then." She covered herself to the waist, then raised her caftan up just enough for him to see her stomach.

Her stomach didn't look so big when she was lying down. "Lucky for you it's only a small watermelon."

"Brant!"

She started to fling down the caftan but he wouldn't let her. "Did the pain go away?"

"It's not really pain. It's more like discomfort." She paused for a second. "There he goes! See!"

Brant knelt and leaned close, seeing a ridge appear to the left of Grace's navel. "What is that?" he demanded.

"Probably a foot. Give it a poke and see."

"A poke!" Brant wasn't going to touch it. He didn't want to hurt her or the baby.

"Like this."

She reached up and gently pressed with one finger. Instantly the ridge went away. Brant sucked in his breath. "How'd you do that?"

"I'm not sure what appendage that is, but if I poke him, he'll stick it back out in a minute. I say I'm playing tag with him."

"You're probably poking him in the eye," Brant said worriedly. "My son's going to have his eyes gouged out by his own mother."

Grace laughed, and the ridge reappeared. "You try."

Tentatively he reached out with a forefinger to touch her. Electricity shot through him as he felt the firmness of Grace's naked belly. He touched the ridge, and it went away like magic. The wonder of it made Brant spread his entire palm over the place where the ridge had been. Grace lay completely motionless as he experienced the first moment of awe. "Where did he go?" he whispered hoarsely.

"I don't know," Grace whispered back. "Maybe he was so comforted by the feel of your hand that he's going back to sleep."

Brant's mouth went dry. His throat felt as if it were tight elastic. Grace's huge hazel eyes watched him with the pride of her motherhood shining from them.

There was only one thing he could say through the thick cotton of his emotions. "Grace Barclay, I'm going to have to marry you, aren't I?"

Chapter Seven

Grace pulled her caftan back over her stomach. Brant's expression was so stunned, so amazed and so afraid. She wished he hadn't said it, but it was best to head off the question he'd voiced. "No, Brant, you're not going to *have* to marry me."

He rocked back on his heels, then moved to sit on the other bed. "I don't see any other way around this, do you?"

"I told you on Sunday that the last thing I wanted was to marry you," she said quietly.

"Yeah, but—" He swept a hand through his dark hair, tousling it. "You didn't mean that."

"Why wouldn't I have meant it?"

His face held wary confusion. "Because that's why we broke up in the first place. Now, I'm willing to marry you."

"That was a long time ago, Brant. A lifetime ago for me." She held up a hand at the protest he was about to make. "I had a lot of time to think while you were gone, Brant. You had every chance in the world to ask me to marry you, but instead you left. You wouldn't have even called me or come to see me once you returned to Fairhaven. If you hadn't come in to get Cami's dress, you wouldn't be here right now.'' She met his hard blue stare. ''There really isn't much left to say about this, Brant.''

''I think there is.'' He got up, pacing the length of the room before turning. ''Grace, it's not fair to the baby for us not to get married.''

''It's not fair to the baby if we *do*.'' She leveled him with her eyes. ''I simply don't see marriage as a reasonable alternative.''

''How can you say that! Marrying Kyle Macaffee *is* a reasonable alternative?'' His tone was thunderstruck.

''I'm not going to marry Kyle.'' Grace dropped her gaze to stare at the peach and green coverlet on the bed. ''I...was considering it. Maybe I would have, but your intrusion into my life has basically ended that course of action.''

''I should think so!''

''Not because of any feelings I might have for you,'' she said waspishly, ''but mainly because you won't go away. It would be too hard on me to have divided loyalties between two men. For now, I think it's best that I tell Kyle you and I are going to have to see how our lives work together where this baby is concerned.''

''Well, that's more like it,'' he said begrudgingly.

''But I'm not entertaining any thought of marrying you, either.'' She was definite on this point. ''And none of your hard-driving, stubborn tactics will change my mind, so you can quit sneaking into my house and following me on business trips.''

''I can't help being worried about you, Grace.''

''You don't have the right. The baby is your concern, true, but I want it understood that as far as you and I go, there is no plan for anything more than what we've got at this moment. Which is a baby's future, and nothing else."

"I don't believe you mean this."

"I do. A bridal bouquet and a gold wedding band couldn't begin to fix what was wrong with our relationship, Brant. I had time to realize that while you were away. Plenty of time."

"You're bitter because I left. You're still angry, and keeping me hostage for my refusal to marry you before."

She shook her head emphatically. "No. You're still not proposing to me. You don't really want to marry me. It's the baby, essentially, that you're proposing to." Her gaze softened for a moment. "Believe me, Brant, one thing you have convinced me of in the past few days is your commitment to this child. You'll be a good father. For a man who's totally lost when it comes to the concept of baby supplies, baby clothes, whatever, you have made a good stab at trying to figure it all out. But it's all for the baby."

"It's not all for the baby. I want to help you, too."

"I know. I appreciate that. But it's not enough to build a marriage on."

"How do you know what's enough? How did you know that what you thought was enough before to build a marriage on would have been enough in twenty years?" His voice was strained, his expression haunted.

She had no good answer for him. "All I can tell you is what I feel. And I feel that you're not in love with me."

"I...I do love you, Grace."

He struggled to say the words, so she tried to be gentle with her response. "You're not *in* love with me, Brant. And while I have genuine feelings of love and affection for you, I don't think I can share anything of myself with you."

Not anymore. She didn't say it, but somehow, the words were clearer because she hadn't.

"You didn't used to feel that way. What's changed, Grace?"

Again, her eyes slid away from his. "My body, for one thing. I could never let you see me naked, and I'm assuming that's a part of being married."

"I'd love to see you naked! I mean, I'd have to."

He'd definitely perked up. Grace laughed, a little wistfully. "Brant, it's so hard to explain. When we…broke up, it was because you didn't see a future for us, a future with me. That's rejection, plain and simple. To a woman, it's like being told 'I don't want you enough to marry you,' or 'You're not the woman of my dreams.' If I wasn't what you wanted when I was slim and at a more attractive state, how do you honestly think I can feel comfortable letting you see me with overlarge, sagging breasts, stretch marks and cellulite I didn't know I had?"

He didn't say anything.

Grace shook her head. "I don't feel beautiful, or desirable anymore. If I wasn't enough for you before, I surely can't be the way I am now. And rumor has it the bod goes downhill from here."

"Grace, I—"

She waved him silent. "Let me give you another thing that's changed. I'm not myself. I don't know who I am sometimes. One day, I was salting a tomato to eat, and for some reason, I burst into tears. I don't even know why. Tears just poured out of my eyes, and to this day, I don't know what upset me.''

"Jeez. If a tomato can make you cry, I'm in a boatload of trouble."

Refusing to smile at him, she said, "Exactly my point."

He paced one more length, then crossed his arms over his chest. "I can handle stretch marks, and I don't care about mood swings—as long as you quit crying eventually. That kind of stuff wouldn't make me not care about you. It's certainly no reason not to marry me."

It was irritating that she couldn't make him see what was so clear to her. Sitting up and arranging a pillow behind her back, Grace shot him an impatient glare. "It's two good reasons to me, but let me give you the third and most important. Your proposal, if one could call it that, was so begrudging, it felt like a donkey was straining to pull it out of you. 'I'm going to have to marry you, aren't I?' are not exactly the words of a man who wants to get married." She eyed him malevolently for a moment. "I've dressed expectant brides who were thrilled to be going down the aisle because their man had finally proposed. They thought everything was going to work out just fine. Then that little baby comes along, bringing with it responsibility, and the men realize that past the initial 'doing the right thing,' they're in a place they didn't want to be."

"I've never had a problem handling responsibility."

"You left Cami to take care of the ranch for three months, Brant! And now you're here in New York, and who's taking care of the ranch again but your pregnant sister!''

"I believed the ranch could wait two days. This is more important to me.'' His gaze was angry, his voice indignant.

"The baby is, Brant.'' Grace sighed. "I'm going to sleep now. I'm exhausted.'' She hesitated, uncomfortable, as he obviously was. "Can we just forget we had this conversation?''

"Can *you?*''

"I don't know.'' She reached up to turn off her lamp. "Good night, Brant.''

He didn't say anything. A moment later, his boots hit the floor with a thump. The covers were jerked off the other bed. Thick silence curtained the room. Grace closed her eyes tightly, refusing to let her heartbreak spill over.

"I DON'T EVEN WANT TO THINK about the return trip, Maggie.'' Grace sat in the Yellowjacket Cafe the next evening, appreciative of the sympathetic ears listening to her story. Tilly had put a plate of steamed vegetables and fried chicken in front of her, but Grace barely picked at the food. "Brant and I hardly said a word to each other.''

"Well, I'm not sure if there was anything left for the two of you to talk about. It's clearly an impasse.''

"It's clearly *impossible*,'' Tilly said, defining the matter further.

Grace had walked over to the Cafe after the dinner rush, so she could enjoy the luxury of having her two friends to herself for another moment. Buzz and Purvis were sitting in their customary places, but they were engrossed in checkers. "What am I going to do?"

"Wait it out, I guess," Maggie said slowly. "Seeing as how you feel the way you do, what else is there?"

Tilly nodded. "Marry in haste, divorce at leisure."

"Tilly!" Maggie exclaimed.

"No. It's all right." Grace sipped some tea. "Tilly has put her finger on exactly what's bothering me. Brant was certainly in no hurry to marry me before, when he had all the time in the world. What good can come out of rushing now? The ink would hardly be dry on the marriage certificate before he might realize being tied to me wasn't what he wanted for the rest of his life."

Maggie and Tilly were silent, gazing at her with distressed eyes.

"I don't want to get married impetuously, then have Brant want a divorce. Or worse yet, stay with me and hate me for it." She touched light fingers to her stomach. "What kind of a way is that for a child to grow up?"

"I don't know," Maggie said on a heavy exhalation of breath. She patted Grace's hand. "I'm not saying a child doesn't need a father, honey. But I am saying that he'll get plenty enough love with you to mother him. Maybe that's more than some kids ever get."

"That's right." Tilly cracked her gum resolutely. "You listen to Maggie. She's a pillar of salt."

Grace giggled. "Like Lot's wife who sneaked a peak at Gomorrah burning?"

"Yep," Maggie replied. "Except what I see is some good people who love each other, but maybe not at the right time, right place in their lives. Give it time, Grace. Everything may yet turn out for the best.''

''I hope you're right.''

The cowbell on the door handle jangled as it opened.

''Howdy, Kyle!'' Maggie called.

''Hi, Maggie, Tilly.'' His eyes settled on Grace. ''Hi, Grace.''

''Hi, Kyle.'' She patted the seat next to her and he joined her.

''Hungry?'' Maggie asked.

''I'd appreciate a glass of tea,'' he said, his eyes only for Grace.

''I'll get it,'' Tilly said softly, leaving the table. Maggie melted away, too, leaving Kyle and Grace alone together.

''How was your trip, Grace?''

She smiled into Kyle's brown eyes, flattered by the admiration she saw there. Yet it made her sad, too. ''It was fine, I guess. I'm glad you stopped by. I...I need to talk to you.''

It was hard to hold his gaze. Grace felt so awful. What she had to say to Kyle was going to hurt him.

He sighed heavily. ''I think I know what the subject matter is.'' Hesitating as he searched her face, he said, ''It's over, isn't it?''

She closed her eyes, turning away for a moment. ''I'm sorry, Kyle.'' Forcing herself to look in his eyes again, she said, ''I care about you a lot. Part of me really thought marrying you might be the best thing to do.''

''But with Brant back in town...''

She hated every second of this conversation.

"Yes. It does make matters more complex. Not that Brant and I are close to working anything out, but it's difficult for me to feel caught in the middle. I'm sorry." Gently she reached to cover his hand with hers. "I just need this time to gather my wits for being a single mother."

"I knew this was coming," Kyle said sorrowfully. "I went around to Brant's ranch to apologize for the altercation on the airplane." A slight smile turned up his mouth. "Brant and I have been agreeable friends over the years. I don't like to be on anybody's bad side unnecessarily, and I figured I was as much at fault for what happened as he was."

"Oh, Kyle, that was nice of you," Grace murmured.

"Yeah." He chuckled disparagingly. "Only Cami told me Brant had gone to New York. That's when I knew the sneaky devil was determined to win you at all costs. I can't blame him for that."

She started to apologize, but he dismissed her with a wave. "It's okay, Grace. My pride was stung at first, but then I thought about it, and decided you're better off with Brant pursuing you if he aims to make everything right for you and the baby. A family should be together."

"Well, I'm not sure what's going to happen in the future, to be honest. We didn't get along so well in New York. Right now, we've left it at the fact that he can see the baby when he's born. In the meantime, I want peace in my life." She scrunched her face apologetically. "I hope you understand."

"I do." Kyle got to his feet, dropping a light kiss on her hair. "Tell Maggie I'll catch that glass of tea later. I'm gonna go home and lick my wounds."

"Oh, Kyle—"

"Teasing, Grace. I'm just teasing."

She could tell by the pain in his eyes that he wasn't. Sadly she watched Kyle say goodbye to Buzz and Purvis as he left the Cafe. The baby kicked, making Grace jump. She put a hand over him, disturbingly aware that he was the only man in her life right now.

"WHAT'S THIS?" Cami glanced at Brant suspiciously. She was sitting in the kitchen, adding up some totals with a calculator.

Brant had laid the box close to her arm, hoping she might not notice right away. Making his peace offering without having to offer any words of apology would have been the easy way out. Not admirable, of course, but he knew Cami was going to let him have it with both barrels loaded.

"It's a little something I picked up in New York. For the baby," he clarified.

"Oh?" Cami's eyebrows jumped to the top of her forehead.

"Can you just open the box without acting like it's a bomb?" he demanded testily.

"I'm sorry, Brant. I didn't realize you were interested in the baby. Did you have an epiphany in New York?"

"Cami," he growled.

"Okay." She reached for the box, taking the lid off. With an expression of amazement for his benefit, she lifted the outfit from the box. "My goodness, Brant, this is almost cute." She looked at the little denim jean and red bandanna shirt for a moment. "Grace picked this out, didn't she?"

"No," he said gruffly. "But she did point out that I haven't congratulated you on the baby, Cami. I apologize for what I said to you, and Dan."

"Well." Cami looked as if a brief wind might knock her over. "Apology accepted, as far as I'm concerned. You might smooth over the waters with Dan when you get a chance. Maybe even welcome him into the 'bosom' of the family."

"Cami!" Brant's tone was brisk. "Don't push me."

She laughed. "I couldn't resist picking at you."

"You've never held back before. I wouldn't expect you to start now." Brant sat at the table across from her, trying to wade his way through these deep waters. He really did want Cami to know that he'd rethought her situation. "By the way, do you know what you're having yet?"

"No. Dan and I want to be surprised."

"Isn't finding out you're having a baby enough of a surprise?"

She laughed merrily. "It certainly knocked you out of whack."

He thumped a palm on the table, unable to disagree. Brant couldn't remember the last time he'd been tied in this many knots.

"Were you and Grace able to come to any reasonable agreement?" she asked gently.

"No." He bit the inside of his mouth for a moment. "I'm not sure that I didn't manage to make everything worse."

"Uh-oh. You did work on your medieval thought processes, didn't you, brother?"

"I think so." He wasn't sure, but he knew he'd tried.

"And you did keep your foot out of your mouth? No smart aleck, chauvinistic remarks, right?"

"Cami, I really tried to be open to new suggestions. And I tried not to get into Grace's way. Too much, anyway."

"Sum this up for me. Give me the moment you realized the two of you weren't sharing the same vision."

That was easy. "When she wanted to put a dress on my son."

Cami laughed. "That doesn't sound like Grace. Was it pretty?"

"Yeah, I guess. Hey! You're not going to tell me that's the latest trend for boys, are you? 'Cause I can tell you, my son's not even going to get an earring when he's a teenager. Or a tattoo, either."

"Right. Your boy's gotta toe the line." Cami made her voice gruff on purpose, mimicking Brant.

"Yeah. Exactly."

"Okay, so you two disagreed over a dress. That's nothing major."

"It's not?"

"No way. You shout and rant and rave for a while, just to get the testosterone moving around, and Grace listens until she's sick of your idiocy, and then she puts the kid in the dress. That's how it works."

"Cami, does Dan know how you think?"

She giggled, then plain guffawed at him. "Dan wouldn't get all worked up over a christening gown. He's a traditional sort of guy."

"So am I!" Brant was completely lost in Cami's logic. "Let me give you another moment when I knew things weren't going to move into a straight line, then. Grace won't marry me."

"Oh. And that came as a huge shock to you?"

He didn't like the sarcasm in her tone. Raising a forbidding eyebrow at her, he said, "Is there a reason it shouldn't have?"

"Well, let me see. You disappear, then when another man is willing to take on your responsibilities—"

"Cami! Let me stop you right there. I don't want to hear one single word about responsibility, okay? I didn't know Grace was pregnant when I left. If she had told me, it might have changed things."

"Probably would have. You would have done the right thing by her, and made her miserable for the rest of her life because you didn't want to be married. Why does a baby change the equation?"

He stared at her in disbelief. "You sound just like Grace." In fact, it wasn't the first time he'd been struck by how alike the two women were.

"Brant," Cami sighed, "it's not that hard to figure out why she'd feel that way. If I were in her shoes, I'd feel the same."

"You *are* in her shoes, for crying out loud! Why are you beating a path to the altar, and I couldn't drag Grace there with a couple of Clydesdales?"

"I'm happy to be getting married because Dan loves me. And I love him."

"I love Grace."

"Well, *I* knew that." Cami managed to make his statement of love sound like poison. "*You* didn't know that before. So she didn't know it, because you didn't tell her. Suddenly Grace discovers she's having a baby, and you're nowhere to be found. Why would she believe you when you tell her you love her now? Nobody develops true love in the space of a single second." She thought about that for a moment. "Well, Dan and I did, but that's different. He's a forward thinker."

"Oh, for—" Brant glared at his sister. "And I'm not."

"No." Cami shot him a saucy grin. "You're so backward, your face is looking at your—"

"Okay. I've had enough. Thank you kindly for your sisterly support." He shot up from the table, prepared to stalk from the room.

"I guess you'll be at the barbecue my friends are throwing for me on Saturday, brother?"

Pausing, Brant definitely heard the baited hook in Cami's words. "Don't try to get me and Grace together, Cami. She and I have agreed that we'll wait until after the baby's born to see how we feel about anything more between us."

"Oh, I wouldn't dream of trying to throw you two together." Her voice was sweet, her expression saucy. "Thanks for the baby outfit, Brant. You're going to make a wonderful uncle."

He puffed up a little. "Of course I am. Everybody keeps acting like I've got bricks in my head or something, but I've got my good points, too."

Cami laughed, looking back down at the figures she was adding. "You do, Brant. And you're right. Pigheaded stubbornness can be an admirable trait in a man. Guaranteed to win a woman's heart every time." She paused to give him a gleeful grin. "I'll see you in the morning."

Brant wasn't sure what his sister's point was, but as he stomped off up the stairs, he knew her quirky little mind had been making one. Heck, Grace was stubborn, too, as stubborn as any woman he knew, so he wasn't suffering from some dreaded disorder of the personality no one else had.

In fact, now that he thought about it, Cami could be more obstinate than he could. Rubbing his chin thoughtfully, Brant had a lightning strike of disturbing intuition.

Cami and Grace were twins sometimes in the way they viewed life. If Cami could be contrary, Grace was right along with her. He'd kind of thought Grace might reconsider his proposal if he gave her a few days to cool off.

Now that he rethought that strategy—and a few of Cami's choice zingers—Brant realized Grace had no intention of changing her mind.

Chapter Eight

Grace put out the final plate of hors d'oeuvres and glanced around her house. She was proud of the decorations she had thought up for Cami and Dan's bridal barbecue. Taking Cami's colors for the wedding—rose and white—Grace had adorned the dining-room table with a deep rose tablecloth, covering it with a white lace overlay. It draped nicely into the rose-colored bows she'd tied on each of the four corners. Soon, Tilly and Maggie would arrive with the food, and they could all set the serving dishes here. The coffee table in front of the fireplace would serve nicely as a place for guests to put their gifts. She had bought a lovely arrangement of Rubin and Calla lilies with some white roses mixed in for this table.

On the back patio, Grace had set up the portable barbecue grill, and decorated a rectangular table with a cabbage rose-patterned cloth in the same colors. She had set out several soda bottles and pitchers of tea, as well as some brightly colored plastic glasses. Sheriff John had volunteered to be in charge of the grill.

In spite of her organization, and how nice everything looked, Grace had nerves. Taking a deep breath, she stole one more look at herself in the oval mirror in the hallway. Brant had to attend his sister's barbecue. It would be awkward for her, and probably just as much for him. They hadn't left New York on the best of terms, nor had they talked since. To her knowledge, Brant hadn't even stopped in at the Cafe; Maggie hadn't mentioned it if he had.

The doorbell chimed, and Grace went to admit a smiling Maggie and Tilly. "Hi, everyone! I see you've put all our friends to work."

Buzz and Purvis stood behind the two women, loaded down with huge trays of barbecue that they'd unloaded from Maggie's truck. "Put everything in the kitchen, please. All the serving bowls are in there."

Tilly came in, wearing a long, slender dress that emphasized her height. "You've done the place up so nice, Grace."

"Mmm-hmm," Maggie agreed. She was wearing a yellow suit that Grace thought suited her dark skin perfectly. "I hope you haven't worn yourself out. We could have done this at the Cafe."

"I barely did anything. Since you two cooked, I had the fun of decorating. Please, make yourselves at home."

"Does that include this poor stray we found hanging out by your mailbox?" Tilly asked. She tugged Brant in by his arm. "He seems to be waiting for an invitation."

Grace's heart dropped to her Sunday boots. "Brant needs no invitation," she said crisply. "He can start warming the grill up for John."

"We went ahead and cooked the meat at the restaurant.'' Maggie cleared a place on the counter for Purvis to set down a large tray containing olives, pickles and purple onion rings. ''Seemed like it would be easier that way.''

''Okay. We'll still eat on the patio.'' Except that left nothing for Brant to do, and he was obviously as uncomfortable as she felt. He looked nice in black trousers that emphasized his height, and a dark green patterned shirt that somehow brightened the blue in his eyes. Why did she have to be so attracted to him? It wasn't just the fact that he was handsome, nor that the second he stepped into a room, he commanded attention. There was something more that kept this man from being just another good-looking guy.

Maybe it was just Brant. The way he was looking at her made the skin on her arms prickle, as if he was trying to figure out what she was thinking. ''Since there's no grilling to be done, Brant, please just...'' Well, not make himself at home, as she'd instructed everyone else. ''Please, excuse me.''

She hurried off to answer the doorbell. It was Sheriff John, along with Cami and Dan. Grace hugged Cami, and then Dan, and took the gift Sheriff John was holding to set on the coffee table. All the while she was conscious of Brant's eyes on her, watching her every move. Grace went to the refrigerator to get out the corsage she'd bought for Cami.

''Hold still a second, Cami,'' she said. Trying to pin the silly thing on with Brant standing so close by was nerve-racking. Maggie had come from the kitchen with Buzz and Purvis to greet Cami and Dan. Sheriff John and Tilly were standing around watching as well. ''There. I think I managed not to put a huge hole in your blouse. You sure do look nice, Cami.''

Cami smiled at Dan, then back at Grace. ''You do, too, Grace. Doesn't she, Brant?''

He only nodded jerkily, to Grace's distress. Cami meant well, but it would be so much better if all of them wouldn't try so hard to help the situation along.

''DID YOU NOTICE the way those two keep sneaking looks at each other?'' Purvis asked Buzz.

Buzz wiped some barbecue sauce from his mouth. ''Yep. Everybody's noticed. It's only Grace and Brant that think nobody's noticed them doing it.''

''We oughta do something about those two.''

''Like what?''

''I don't know.'' Purvis glanced around the kitchen. ''Hard to get 'em in the same room to talk. Each time one of 'em walks near the other, that'n leaves the room. It's like watching Ping-Pong balls.''

''We could tell 'em something needs their attention on the patio, then lock 'em out. They'd have to talk to each other then.''

Purvis considered that for a moment. ''Don't think it'd work. They'd just walk around the house and let theirselves in the front door. Has to be something more surreptitious.''

He was proud of his fifty-cent word. Buzz didn't appear to notice, and Purvis was disappointed. ''They're gonna have to sit in the same room while Cami and Dan open their presents.''

''So?''

Buzz scratched his head. ''I dunno. They'll be in the same room, at least.''

''It's hard to believe you fought in World War II,''

Purvis said in disgust. "What kind of tactical maneuver is that?"

"Ground control. You gotta have the enemy close together in order to launch an appropriate attack. Same as in checkers, you know."

"I'm beginning to see your point." Purvis could relate to anything that involved checkers. "Get more jumps if the checkers are lined up just right."

"Exactly. Now, here's the plan…"

TEN MINUTES LATER, everyone was seated in the den area, ready to watch Cami and Dan open their shower gifts. Brant was especially uncomfortable with this part of the evening. It reminded him that if Grace would have accepted his proposal, she might be able to celebrate their wedding with her friends, too.

Of course, the plaguing voice mocked him, *if you'd asked her six months ago when she mentioned marriage to you, you wouldn't be feeling like a cowboy who's just been thrown.*

She looked gorgeous. He managed to get a glance every time it was safe to, and he didn't think she'd ever looked more beautiful in all the time he'd known her. The emerald green dress swayed around her ankles, skimming the top of the cream-colored slightly heeled boots she wore. The emerald brought out the silver highlights in her hair and emphasized the hazel of her eyes. The best part, though, was the pinpoint freckles dusted across her nose. They had always been one of his favorite features, and the deep, rich green of her dress brought those to the surface.

Since Grace was still in the kitchen, and he was the only other guest to venture into the den, there were only two seats left, one next to Purvis and one across the room next to Buzz. Brant headed for the one next to Purvis.

As soon as he sat down, the old guy moved across the room to sit in the other available chair. That left the spot next to Brant open, and he saw Grace eye it reluctantly as she came in from the kitchen. Everyone was looking at her innocently—too innocently. Purvis and Buzz sneaked a grin at each other and nodded. Instantly Brant knew he'd been shanghaied by those two checker-loving codgers.

Silently Grace took the chair without a glance at him, and Brant felt his palms begin to sweat. He hoped Cami and Dan would open the presents without delay so he could escape. Much more of pretending as if he and Grace were casual, when her stomach proclaimed they hadn't been in the past, and he was going into seclusion at his ranch until the baby was born.

"IT WAS A LOVELY PARTY, Grace. Thank you."

Cami hugged her, as did Dan. The happy couple left, their car overflowing with gifts. Maggie and Tilly were in the kitchen cleaning up. To Grace's relief, Brant had scooted out to help Dan pack the presents into the car, had waved goodbye at her from the street and promptly taken his truck out of her driveway.

"Well. That was easy with you two doing all the work." Grace came back into the kitchen to discover Maggie and Tilly were in the process of leaving. The sheriff had lingered on the pretext of helping them load up, but Grace knew better. When he could, the sheriff stuck to Maggie as if he were paste.

"I'm glad you let us have the shower here, Grace," Maggie said. "It made for such a cozy gathering. At the Cafe I think we would have all felt like it was just hanging out as usual."

"Well, I was happy to do it."

The three friends looked at each other silently for a moment. "Grace, there's something Maggie and I want to ask you. Actually Cami's in on it, too, but she asked us to go ahead and discuss it with you so she could go on home with Dan." Tilly waited for Grace's nod. "We're hoping you'll let us give you a baby shower."

"Oh." Grace stared at Maggie and Tilly for a second. "Well, that's awfully sweet of you, but—"

"Honey, think about it for a while. Then let us know," Maggie interrupted. "We'd really like to do something for you."

Because there wasn't going to be any wedding showers like the one they'd given Cami and Dan. For the first time, Grace was just a tiny bit envious of the fact that everything was going so well for them. Reprimanding herself, Grace shook her head. "You're both kind to offer. But I can't let you."

"Grace," Maggie said quietly, "that baby's coming in two months."

"Three." Grace corrected her quickly.

"Two." Maggie's tone was stern. "Your due date is August 1. This is the end of May. You've left an entire month off your countdown."

Grace remained silent.

"That baby's coming, no matter what you and Brant decide to do. It's not going to stay in your stomach until the two of you work things out."

Grace walked into the den and sank into a chair. "I don't suppose it will."

"It's time to start getting some things ready." Tilly sat on the chair arm and patted her back. "Have you decided where the baby's going to sleep?"

"In my room," Grace said automatically.

"That'll work for a while, especially if you're going to breast-feed, but what about after that?" Maggie asked.

"The guest bedroom." Grace stared up the stairs in bewilderment. The guest bedroom upstairs at least had a bathroom attached. She had her office in that room, but maybe that should be moved into the bedroom downstairs. She wanted her child close by—

"Okay. Do we need to paint? Wallpaper?" Maggie's approach was methodical.

"I...haven't thought about it." Grace stared down at her fingernails for a second. "I don't suppose the baby cares, do you?"

"Grace." Tilly squeezed her shoulders. "The baby doesn't care. But most new mothers do. We want to help you, if you'd like to decorate a nursery." She glanced at the pretty stuff Grace had set around to create the bridal shower atmosphere for Cami's party. "We know you'd like such, Grace. Let us help you with this."

Tears welled up in Grace's eyes. "I feel silly, leaning on you for help."

"Why?" Maggie demanded. "Grace, what you're facing is difficult. We're in a position to help."

Couldn't she enjoy this support from her friends without feeling guilty? Brant hadn't looked at her all night; he couldn't wait to leave her house. They'd agreed to keep any meetings between them to a minimum until an infant necessitated more contact. Decorating a nursery didn't have to involve Brant.

"I think I'd like that," Grace said softly.

"That's my girl," Maggie said with a quick pat on her hand. "Now, what we'd kinda been thinking on is a nursery shower."

"It sounds interesting," Grace said weakly. "You two always manage to cook up unconventional ideas." She sat up, liking the idea more and more. "I really appreciate you both for this. You'll just never know how much."

"How about Sunday afternoon after church?" Maggie asked.

"Tomorrow! Why so soon?"

"Because," Maggie said sensibly, "this won't take long. Cami, Tilly and I have got this all planned out. Next weekend's the wedding, and Cami and Dan'll be gone for their honeymoon. Then that next weekend already gets us to the middle of June. You haven't bought a crib, nor even enrolled in those classes we're supposed to be in. I'm still your labor coach, aren't I?"

"Yes." Grace hadn't cared to broach the subject to Brant. He was struggling so hard to catch up with basic baby concepts that the idea of trying to explain coaching to him seemed ludicrous.

"I figured as much." Maggie tapped her chin. "We gotta get settled into those classes. By then, it's coming to July, your last month. It'll be hotter than Hades, too hot to paint and such. Might as well do it while we can still let a breeze in."

"I suppose you have a point." Grace couldn't believe she hadn't figured out all of this herself. She was usually so organized, so precise! "I don't know why I haven't been thinking about all this."

"Because you've been busy with plans for Cami, Grace," Tilly said kindly. "Isn't it easier to think of what someone else needs rather than yourself?"

"I...guess." She had bought a few baby outfits in New York. More serious purchases, however, such as a crib, she had put off thinking about, spending all her emotional energy on her business instead. It was the busiest time of the year for her, and plus, she unconsciously avoided slowing down long enough to think out her situation. "The size my stomach's getting should have warned me it was time to start thinking about the baby. But tomorrow! I don't even know what color I want the nursery to be!" Grace was alarmed by the speed with which her friends were planning to convert her office into a real, can't-ignore-it-any-longer baby room.

"Well." Maggie's expression was sheepish. "We didn't think you'd have time, so Tilly and I went to Home Depot and spent an afternoon looking over paint chips and wallpaper borders. Do you mind if we take over this project?"

Grace considered briefly before shaking her head. "I think it would be best if you do. My head is whirling."

"Good." Maggie stood. "Plan on your nursery shower being tomorrow, then, directly after church and the lunch crowd. We've got lots to do."

"It's just going to be the four of us, right?" Grace asked. There wouldn't be time to ask anyone else.

"Not exactly." Tilly's grin was infectious with its slyness. "We were going to surprise you, but decided tonight maybe that wasn't the best idea. A week ago, we invited everybody to come over and get some paint in their hair.''

"Everybody?" Grace couldn't imagine who all cared to paint on their Sunday afternoon off.

"Everybody who was here tonight."

Tears jumped into her eyes. "You're such good friends. What would I do without you?"

Tilly and Maggie glanced at each other hesitantly. "Well, that's that, then," Maggie said too quickly, heading for the door.

"Get your rest," Tilly called gaily. "We're bringing munchies, so don't go shopping, Grace. Just rest, and we'll see you tomorrow."

Tilly pulled the door closed behind her. "Do you think Cami can pull off her part?"

"Of course," Maggie snorted, hopping into the truck and gunning the engine. "When have you ever known Cami *not* to be able to wrap Brant around her little finger?"

Chapter Nine

That night Brant awakened suddenly, his mind teeming with the aftereffects of the most disturbing dream he could ever remember having.

"Why didn't you and Mommy get married, Daddy?"

His eyes opened wide before he rolled over to try to get more comfortable. The question could go unanswered.

"Why, Daddy?"

The little boy voice bothered him again. A face he didn't know but might love one day stared at him inquisitively. Brant exhaled tiredly. "It's hard to explain, son. I'll tell you when you're older."

Wait a minute. Some things you were never old enough to hear—especially from your dad. His father had been his usual self as he unemotionally explained that his wife had left him and that they had decided to get a divorce. There had been no spark of indignation, or even shock. It was as if his mother had never existed for his father, so her absence wouldn't mean anything more than her presence had.

Brant hadn't handled the scene well. "Why?"

he'd wanted to shout at his father. "Why don't you do something?"

"Why? Why?" the little boy voice mocked him. "Why don't you do something, Daddy?"

Brant shot upright in the bed. His heart pounded; his mind's eye saw Grace and her laughing hazel eyes.

How could he ever make his child understand what he didn't even understand himself?

CAMI GLARED AT BRANT mutinously. They had just gotten home from church. He was hungry, he was still tired for some reason and he had a lot to do today. Now his sister was suggesting he accompany her into town to see Grace, which was the last thing he was going to do today. She was the reason he was tired! He hadn't slept a wink last night from thinking about her.

"I am not going, Cami. Besides, Grace will be much happier if I'm not there."

Last night at the barbecue had proved to him that the ornery woman really didn't want to be in his company. She'd spoken two words to him, and no more.

"It's not going to kill you to move some furniture for us, Brant. In fact, it'll be good for you to do some painting. Let out some of the artistic, sensitive side you keep so well hidden."

"No. That's final. It's not open for discussion."

Cami sent an appraising look his way. Brant stiffened, recognizing his sister's churning brain cogs.

"Did you ever get around to calling Mom and breaking the good news?"

"I thought I might this afternoon. I've got a lot of

chores, but it's not fair to wait until she and Grace run into each other at the wedding next weekend.''

"True.'' Cami appeared to consider his words. "What about Dad?''

"What about him?'' Brant demanded. This was a turn he definitely didn't want Cami's brain to take.

"When are you going to tell him?''

"Someday.'' Brant wasn't going to call his father anytime soon. He was a remote man, difficult to talk to. They hadn't shared many heart-to-hearts over the years. Brant saw no reason to start now.

"Of course,'' Cami began casually, "Mom will likely mention it to him this weekend when she and Dad are forced to acknowledge each other's presence.''

"Each other's—'' Brant broke off his words, feeling his gut tighten. It had never occurred to him that his parents might actually end up in the same room together after they'd divorced. "Dad is coming?''

"Yes!'' Cami was indignant. "Who did you think was going to give me away?''

"Me, damn it!''

"*Ohhh*. Brant, I'm sorry.'' Cami looked honestly distressed. "I mean, he is my father. He has to walk me down the aisle.''

Brant crossed his arms, more hurt than he'd care to admit. "I suppose so. I just hadn't thought of it, is all.'' *For the love of heaven. Both of my parents are going to be here this weekend.* "Where are they staying?'' he demanded.

"Here, of course.'' Cami looked at him as if he was crazy. "It *was* their house, once upon a time.''

"Who invited them?''

"I did. Brant! What did you expect? That I'd make them stay in a Motel Six?"

"I don't give a damn! Mother can stay, but our father can stay somewhere else!" Brant's heart hammered in his chest. "Cami, do you think you could have included me in your plans?"

"You weren't here for three months." She bit off the words. "Why are you so upset?"

"Because." Brant stomped out of the room, but Cami followed at his heels. She wouldn't go away, not his sister, until she'd totally messed up his mind. "They got a divorce. They don't need to stay under this roof at the same time."

"Okay. I can tell them the house is full."

"Not Mom. You ought to have her around to help you get dressed or something." Brant didn't know. What he did know was that he was about to bust from what he was hearing.

"Brant." Cami put a soft hand on his arm. He halted, turning slowly to face her. "Let go of it."

"I can't. I can't! They were married nearly thirty years and threw it away just like it never happened." He snorted. "In all that time, the old man couldn't figure out how to be a husband to Mom?"

"Uh, some men are slower than others."

Cami's eyes were trained on him with an expression so intense Brant realized she was lumping him in with his father. "I'm not like him." Just a little, but it wasn't the same at all. "Maybe I am somewhat. But I'll figure it out when the time comes."

"Brother," Cami said slowly, "the time was nearly seven months ago."

He stared at her, angry. Angry with everyone. Angry with himself.

"I've blown it, haven't I?"

"I'm not sure. You scared Grace pretty well when you left. She knew you didn't want to give her anything of yourself. Now the stakes are higher. She wants to be loved for herself, but the baby is what brought you back around to her. Without the baby, would you have ever called her again?"

Caring for her had been way too frightening. How could anyone make a lifetime commitment? "I don't know," he murmured. "I never got over Grace. She is the only woman I've ever cared about."

"But you didn't want to get hurt. I understand, Brant." Cami's eyes clouded. "It hurt when Mom left Dad. It was painful seeing her hurt all those years Dad pretty much left her out of his life. But, Brant, you don't have to be the man Dad is." Her eyes pleaded with him. "Don't you see that? You can let yourself care for Grace. You can show her you do."

"I feel like my brain's dissolving," Brant complained. "Once you start working on me, I actually think you make sense, little sister."

"Good." Cami gave him a playful smack upside the head.

"Where would you suggest I start in my wooing of Grace?" He held his hands up in surrender. "I'm only asking because you seem to have all the answers."

Cami snorted at his sarcasm. "Let's go slap a little paint on her walls and see where that gets you."

He eyed her in disgust. "You did it again. You little she-devil."

She laughed out loud and tweaked his cheek. "You're going to miss me when I'm gone. Don't say I didn't warn you."

He already missed her. In fact, he missed a lot of things. After the soul-wrecking dream he'd had last night, Brant was beginning to fear missing even more.

GRACE CAME HOME from church, where she'd missed most of the sermon while she was cautiously sliding her vision to Brant, who sat about ten pews away. Her feelings were a little bruised, and she realized she had wanted him to sit with her. She wanted to see him—in spite of all her protestations otherwise.

It had felt so awkward sitting in church, but not being together. Somehow, Grace felt as if they were cheating the baby.

Afterward, she had not seen him. Though they'd agreed to this arrangement, it was still difficult. Grace skipped going to the Cafe for Sunday brunch and hurried home instead. Taking off her dress and Sunday shoes, she changed into some maternity shorts and a loose top. Catching sight of herself in the mirror, Grace thought, *The fewer clothes I have on, the less attractive I am.* Definitely her belly protruded more in shorts than when she wore a dress.

No matter, she decided. For painting a room, shorts were a must. Grace yawned, curling up on the bed to indulge in a short catnap.

Two hours later, the doorbell chimed, startling her awake. "Maggie!" she exclaimed, aghast that she hadn't been getting anything ready for her guests. Flying down the stairs, Grace opened the door. Her apologies died on her lips at the sight of Cami and Brant standing on the porch.

"Hi. Come in," she told them, her eyes fastened

to Brant's face. Why was Brant here? She ran a hand through sleep-tangled hair, dismayed.

"Are you all right, Grace?" Cami peered at her closely. Brant's gaze was just as concerned.

"I'm fine. I fell asleep for a while," she said sheepishly. "You two sit down and make yourselves comfortable."

Brant's eyes were pinned to her stomach. Grace backed away, mortified. "I'm going to run upstairs for a minute. Cami, please play hostess if anyone else arrives."

She flew to her room and snatched up a hairbrush. Maggie hadn't mentioned that Brant was going to help decorate the nursery. What did Brant know about wallpaper and curtains?

Quickly she brushed her hair, teeth and washed sleep from her eyes. She dabbed the slightest bit of perfume under her hair, before realizing it was too hot to work without her hair in a ponytail. Swiftly she pulled her hair back.

Her gaze dropped to her stomach. No doubt about it: The baby was definitely announcing his presence now. All this beautifying for Brant couldn't disguise her condition. If she was hoping to make Brant aware of her as a woman, she was dreaming. He couldn't be aware of anything but her pregnancy. Downhearted, Grace rejoined her guests.

"Are you sure you're up to this, Grace?" Cami asked.

"Yes. I don't know why I fell asleep like that. I was just going to close my eyes for twenty minutes." She couldn't look at Brant.

"I've been tired more myself," Cami replied. "The baby makes me want naps in the afternoon."

She shot Brant an impish grin. "I'll be glad to go on my honeymoon so I can leave all the ranch chores to Brant."

The doorbell chimed, saving Brant from his sister's teasing. Grace noted he seemed distinctly surprised to hear Cami say she was tired more lately.

On the porch, she found Sheriff John and Maggie. Buzz and Purvis lurked behind them, while Tilly was walking up the sidewalk with what appeared to be bags from the grocery store.

"Come on in, everybody," Grace called, trying to let them know by the sound of her voice how much she appreciated them coming to help her with the nursery. The last thing she wanted was for anyone to know how much seeing Brant had unsettled her. Her gaze narrowed on the giant box John was carrying. "Party supplies?"

"Nope." He carried the box inside and sat it in front of Brant.

"Open it, Grace," Maggie told her. "It's just a little something for the baby."

"I thought decorating the nursery was for the baby." Grace tried to make her voice stern, but she could feel tears tickling the back of her eyes. Her friends were too good to her.

"Honey, it isn't a baby shower without a present. Go ahead and open it. Brant, you take one end and Grace, you get the other."

Grace eyed the pink giraffe and blue elephant wrapping paper with some trepidation. The box was too large to contain a bib. She forced herself to meet Brant's eyes over the box. Her heart was pounding uncomfortably; she felt herself perspiring. The last thing she'd ever envisioned was opening baby gifts

with Brant Durning. All their friends were looking
on with indulgent smiles, so Grace swallowed her
uneasiness. "On the count of three," she told him
with her brightest, let's-get-this-over-with smile.
"One, two, three!"

He pulled one end, she pulled the other to reveal
a brown box. Brant slit the tape on the box, and
gestured for her to look. Grace peered into the box.

A jumbo-size, white-woven bassinet basket lay inside.

Grace burst into tears.

"What is it, Grace, honey?" Maggie asked, glancing at Brant in bewilderment.

Tears slid down Grace's cheeks as she shook her
head. Buzz and Purvis shifted uncomfortably.

Brant took a quick look inside the box. "I think
this is a tomato kind of moment. Grace is just surprised."

"Oh," Cami murmured, as if she understood.

"I don't know why I'm crying. I'm happy!"
Grace wailed. "You're all doing too much for me. I
just don't know how to say thank you. This is the
most beautiful thing I've ever seen."

Tilly pulled a tissue off a table and handed it to
her. "We're glad you like it. We weren't sure what
to get. We figured you'd want to pick out your own
crib and baby furniture."

"Why don't you take it upstairs so we can get the
boys working?" Maggie suggested.

Grace wiped her eyes and stood. "Are you sure
you want to do this? The bassinet is more than
enough."

"We've come to fix a nursery and that's what
we're gonna do," John said. "This may be the only

time you've got five strong men here to move stuff, Grace. Point the way.''

IN THIRTY MINUTES, the men had Grace's office moved downstairs. It occurred to Brant that she was having to do an awful lot of changing in a lot of different ways. Other than trying to get his feelings sorted out, Brant was just trying to get up to speed with this baby business, but he hadn't been inconvenienced in any way. He intensely disliked the sensation that Grace was doing this pregnancy all by herself.

He hated feeling remote, absolutely detested it. Yet, there didn't seem to be any way for him to be more included.

"All right. Now we're down to the tacks,'' Maggie said with satisfaction. "Guys, unscrew the light plates, et cetera. Tilly, start stirring the paint. Brant and Grace, go find yourselves something to do.''

"Do!'' Grace glanced at Brant sharply. "I've got to help with the painting.''

"Uh-uh. Ain't good for a pregnant woman to smell paint fumes.''

"Oh, for heaven's sake! You said we had to do this project this weekend so the window could be open to let in a breeze. I'll be fine.''

"Nope.'' Sheriff John took her by the shoulder and gently showed her to the door. "Not taking any chances. Besides, we got too many people in here, and you two'll be underfoot. And Maggie and Tilly's wanting their decorating to be a surprise, so no peeking till we're finished. Brant, why don't you help Grace set up the bassinet?''

He realized he'd been outmaneuvered again.

Sourly Brant hoped Grace didn't think he'd been a party to this plan. What was there to putting together a bassinet, for crying out loud? "All right," he replied, disgruntled, "though my painting skills would come in handy."

He'd left the box with the bassinet in it in Grace's bedroom to get it out of the way. Following her down the hall, Brant eyed her. "I think we're victims of well-meaning friends."

"Let's just make the best of it." Her voice was so crisp, Brant knew Grace was as uncomfortable as he was.

"Fine." Carefully he pulled the basket from the box and set it on Grace's double bed. "Looks small laying there like that." He squinted at the print on the box. "Says it's jumbo-size, though."

Grace couldn't take her eyes off the basket. "I love the wicker look," she said softly. "I bet it cost a fortune."

He glanced inside the box again. "Well, here's the wheels so baby can go coasting at his option." Pulling the rest of the contraption out, Brant put the basket on top of the frame, assembling the screws that held it together. "What're you going to do with this thing, anyway?"

"I guess I'll keep it by my bed, so that when the baby gets up in the night to breast-feed, I'll have him close by."

Brant paused. "Breast…feed?"

A pink blush crept up Grace's neck. "Well, yes. What did you think?"

Brant wasn't sure. "That he'd drink out of a bottle?" How in the hell was he going to be a part of any of his baby's life if he couldn't even hold him in his arms to give him a bottle?

"I'd like to give breast-feeding a try. It's better for the baby."

He kept his eyes on the screw he was attaching. "I'm sure it is." Breasts were great for males of any age. Wisely he refrained from offering any assistance in that department. It sounded as if the baby would have his own efficient, self-serve operation.

"What's that supposed to mean?"

Brant barely glanced up, but he saw that Grace had her hands on her hips. "Nothing. Don't get all heated up with me, Grace, because I hardly know what you're talking about. I guess I just thought I'd be able to help out with the baby some." He couldn't look at her. The screw was well in place, so Brant abandoned trying to act busy.

"Well, there'll be something you can do, Brant. I promised not to leave you out, and I meant it." She looked to make sure they hadn't left any pieces that went with the bassinet inside the box. "Oh, my goodness," she murmured.

"What?" What else could Maggie and Tilly and crew have put in the treasure chest Grace was digging through?

"Look." She pulled out a lacy cloth bumper, a tiny pillow and a package of sheets. "Oh, it's going to be so darling!"

Brant watched as Grace began tying the bumper inside the bassinet. Little white satin bows appeared through the wicker. He swallowed, seeing how happy all this made her. What could he do that would bring that same smile to Grace's face?

"Cami and Dan signed up for some baby classes,"

he said hesitantly. "He's going to be her labor coach.
I can only guess at what all that entails, but…" He
paused as Grace's head came up, her eyes wary as
her fingers stilled on the ribbons. "Would you like
for me to be your labor coach?"

By the astonished, rather unhappy expression on
her face, Brant knew the answer was no. Immediately
confusion swept him.

"Maggie's going to be my labor coach." Grace
got busy with the bows again. "Thank you for offering."

Her voice was crisp again, and Brant knew there
was no sincere gratitude behind her polite thank-you.
He stared down at his hands, seeing the cracks and
chapped skin of a working man. What was there to
give Grace that she didn't already have?

How was he ever going to show her that he cared?

Chapter Ten

Grace shot Brant a nervous glance. She could feel him struggle with their situation. Offering him a tentative smile, she suddenly froze when his hands wrapped around her wrists and gently tugged her closer, a move she in no way resisted.

"Grace," he whispered, "you're shutting me out."

She hesitated, staring up into his eyes. "Maybe a little."

He gave a small grunt. "Maybe a lot. I know you had to do a lot of thinking about this baby on your own, but it's not that way anymore. We said we'd wait until after the baby's born to see how we feel about getting married, but I can't wait any longer to do this." Without hesitation, he molded his mouth to hers.

Grace closed her eyes on a sigh at the feel of Brant's lips on hers. A million old-new emotions sizzled through her. He felt so good! This man she loved, how could she tell him no about anything?

The next second, he'd sat on the bed, pulling her onto his lap. His palms captured the side of her face, his lips meeting hers, pressing, demanding, again and again. Grace sighed with sublime happiness and wrapped her arms around his neck. It was sheer heaven to be in his arms again. She had dreamed of this moment for the six months she'd known it to be impossible. Her eyes closed, she let her other senses work: Her fingers told her his skin was just as rough at the neckline as ever, his hair just as soft, his shoulders just as broad. She could smell aftershave and soap and clean-washed shirt. The taste of him as their tongues met reminded her forcefully that only this man had ever made her want to drown in his love.

The past slid away for the moment, until suddenly, unfortunately, they were both out of breath. Pulling away, Grace tried to avoid meeting Brant's eyes. She succeeded, for a moment.

"Grace," he said huskily, "you're beautiful."

No, she wasn't, but she was shaking like crazy at what she'd just done. "You're awfully proud of your handiwork."

He laughed a little. "I am at that. Amazed, to be honest. The fact that there's a little person growing inside of you—well, it leaves me without words. But Cami's pointed out that I'm without words most of the time." He took her chin in his fingers and pulled it up so that she had to look into his eyes. "I've always thought you were beautiful, ravishing, sexy. I wish I'd told you before."

"Just because you're getting out of wallpapering and painting doesn't mean you should go overboard." She gave him a mock stern look. "You might say something you'll regret later."

"I hope not. I don't want to hurt you ever again."

She smiled at him, a hopeful, trying-to-be-brave smile, before he lay back on the bed, pulling her with him. Snuggling her head in the crook of his shoulder and enjoying the small circles he was smoothing over her back, Grace wondered if this could really be happening. The white lace canopy hung overhead, as it had many other afternoons they'd lain together, and Grace told herself not to expect too much. This moment together was just a beginning.

BUZZ PEEKED into the bedroom, his mouth agape at the sight of Grace and Brant entwined in each other's arms. He sped back into the nursery.

"I don't think Grace cares to bring us any munchies and drinks right now." His chest bunched out with pride when he caught everyone's immediate attention. "Her and Brant's sound asleep on the bed."

A delighted gasp erupted in the room. Tilly clapped her hands together. "Our plan is working!"

Maggie held up a hand. "Are they asleep on the same side of the bed?"

Buzz nodded importantly. "Wrapped around each other like cotton on a swab."

"Guess putting together a baby bassinet's hard work," Purvis interjected.

Sheriff John laid down his paintbrush. "Well, now what?"

"You take Buzz and Purvis downstairs and help them set up a tray if you can find one. Bring some sodas and chips and whatever else Tilly had, and we'll have us a celebration!" Maggie picked up her paintbrush again, giving the wall under her supervision an approving glance. "This is going very well, if I do say so myself."

BRANT SHIFTED AWAY from Grace, as much as he hated doing it. The way she'd been sleeping, ever so trustingly, against his shoulder had given him hope for their relationship. Memories of the way things had been before…before the marriage question.

The question was no longer a point, of course. His bachelor brain had not been able to bear thinking about getting married last fall. Now, he knew it was something that had to be done, for many reasons. He might have taken down the first chunk in Grace's wall of resistance, but how to get past it altogether?

Somehow, he knew she'd be uncomfortable to wake up and find him still sleeping with her. They hadn't meant to fall asleep together, and the fact that it had happened so innocently was wonderful. Still, at this point on the game board, he didn't want to be told to return to square one. She could be mighty determined, and if she said she wasn't marrying him, then she meant just that. He wasn't going to push.

Touching his finger softly to her cheek and pulling a quilt over her legs, Brant said softly, "It ain't over till it's over, Grace Barclay." It was a vow of a different kind, and he could be just as determined as she could.

He walked into the nursery, surprising Maggie so badly she dropped her paintbrush. "Dang it, Brant! It's a good thing we put down a drop cloth, or there'd be white paint on this ice blue rug. What are you doing in here, anyway?"

Brant eyeballed the seven pairs of eyes sternly reproving him. "We finished putting the basket together." He jammed his hands into his jeans and tried not to give away what he'd really been doing.

"Looked like you quit on the basket and started

in on the bed,'' Buzz said offhandedly. His near-toothless grin told Brant that everyone knew he'd been napping with Grace.

"Grace was tired,'' he lied, but everyone booed him. He laughed at their good-natured teasing. "Shh! Don't tell anyone, but she might be thawing on me.'' His antennae quivered as he darted a nervous glance over his shoulder. If Grace ever heard him say something like that, she'd stay at the south end of the thermometer with him!

"Sunday naps just get better once you're married,'' Maggie teased.

"How the hell would you know?'' Brant shot back.

Her eyes widened, but she didn't look John's way. "I...I reckon I just heard that somewhere.'' She cleared her throat.

"As a matter of fact,'' Brant said, allowing his eyes to slowly rove the room face by face, "there isn't a married soul in here.''

"Been married, though,'' Buzz offered.

"Yeah? How was it?'' Brant demanded.

"Sunday naps get ya through the rest of the week.'' He grinned hugely.

Buzz's wife—and Purvis's, too—had passed away many years ago, which was, Brant supposed, how the two happened to have so much in common with each other. Neither seemed interested in finding another woman, and they had to be getting on to seventy, or older—

His speculative eye lit on his sister and Dan. "I don't want to hear about your Sunday naps. Somehow, I think that's why I'll be standing at the altar next weekend.''

"You must like those naps, too, brother," Cami snapped back. "And apparently, you learned to like 'em a lot sooner than I did."

Laughter exploded. He could feel the back of his neck burning. "That leaves you, John."

"Don't drag me into this. Maggie and me, we don't take naps. We're too young and full of energy."

The sheriff grinned at the round owner of the Cafe. Maggie sniffed and slapped a roll of wallpaper boarder into his hand. "See if you have enough energy to start prepasting that." To Brant, she said, "We might none of us be married...yet—" she nodded toward Cami and Dan "—but we've got plenty of good advice for you."

"Such as?"

"You got lipstick on your mouth."

A red flush burned his face. Brant rubbed his mouth impatiently, unable to meet any of their interested faces. Every last one of them was holding back a snicker, and if they weren't people he'd known forever, he'd feel more stupid than he already did. "That's the best advice you've got?" he demanded.

"Nah. That ain't advice. It's a fact," Maggie said placidly. "The advice is to take your butt into a jewelry store, Brant, and get Grace something she can't tell you no over." Maggie's eyes trained on him with pointed amusement. "Ain't that your problem? She won't make an honest man of ya?"

The laughter was back in the room. Brant bit the inside of his cheek. A jewelry store! He'd rather walk barefoot over bamboo shoots.

"Now, if you're shy, Dan oughta be able to show you the ropes." Maggie pointed with another roll of wallpaper to a glass that was sitting on the makeshift worktable. "There, in that glass so it won't get paint on it, is the token of her lover's esteem."

"Maggie," Brant growled. He didn't want to be reminded too much of how Dan had gotten Cami the way she was. Glancing at his sister, he saw the crestfallen expression on her face and realized she wanted him to go look. Whatever was in that damn glass meant an awful lot to her. Trying not to feel as if he was about to examine an insect in a bottle, Brant advanced on the glass.

"Wow!" he said, pulling the ring from its resting place. "Must be good money in horses, Dan." The diamond in it was huge! Brant couldn't imagine putting so much money into—instantly, he warned himself to slow down. Dan appeared to be doing everything right for Cami. She was having a—what had Purvis called it?—a hoedown? at the Double D. Grace had specifically helped Cami select a gown and veil—no cutting corners on the dream-come-true stuff there. And a honeymoon to a romantic destination was topping the whole marriage off…maybe he'd better change his way of thinking. If Grace ever relented on having him, he'd need something like the sparkly thing he was gingerly holding between his fingers to give her.

"It's nice, Cami," he said, dropping it back into the glass. He couldn't force the question he wanted to ask onto his tongue.

"Thanks, Brant," Cami said softly, something akin to sisterly pity in her eyes.

"I got it at the jewelry store on the square," Dan said kindly. "Mr. Carpenter won't gouge you like the city stores try to."

"Oh." Brant acted nonchalant, as if he wasn't filing away where the ring had come from for future reference. "Well, what do you want me to help with, Maggie?"

She looked suspicious at his abrupt change of subject. "Well, since you and John are the tallest, you can start slappin' up that border. But you ain't supposed to be in here," she reminded him. "This is part of your wedding—I mean, baby gift from us."

He ignored her slip, which he felt was halfway on purpose, and got up on the stepladder. "I know nothing about putting up border," he complained.

"And you know nothing about women, either," Maggie replied, sticking a brush and a flat-edged piece of plastic into his hand. "By this time next week, you'll have gone through a crash course. I hope you survive it."

Brant laughed at Maggie's ribbing, because he had to be a good sport. He thought about Grace asleep and soft and warm down the hall. So much was changing so fast, for now all he could do was hang on and try to pass the course.

GRACE AWAKENED, hearing voices carrying down to her room. She stretched, then halted immediately as she remembered how she'd gotten where she was. Brant had been kissing her as if there was no tomorrow. Somewhat chagrined, she remembered that the feel of being in his arms again had been more like there had only been yesterdays between them. The yesterdays before they'd broken up...she reflexively touched her lips in wonder. Her heart aching, Grace knew that she still loved Brant with all her soul. The baby bassinet stood white and beribboned in the waning afternoon sunlight, and Grace pushed herself to her feet. It was humiliating enough that she'd fallen asleep when she should be acting the part of a good hostess. No point in cowering in her bedroom, even if it was going to be awfully hard to look into Brant's eyes.

He couldn't be fooled by her coolness anymore. Brant Durning knew he had her heart, body and soul—which was a dangerous position for her to be in.

"I'm awake!" she called down the hall, loud enough to startle someone into slamming the nursery door closed.

"Don't come in!" someone shrieked.

Grace grinned. That panicked yell sounded like Maggie. "Anybody thirsty, or hungry?" Grace called through the door.

"No, but we're sleepy!" Cami called back.

Grace laughed. "Since I'm awake now, I can play hostess like I should have been doing all along."

"Just cool your jets, Grace!" Maggie's tone had Grace smiling. "Stay right where you are. We'll be out in a sec."

Whispering erupted on the other side of the door. Grace ran a hand through her hair, satisfied that the ponytail holder was still on. A quick glance at herself in the mirror was in order, however, especially since Brant had kissed her. She wanted to look nice, in case the opportunity presented itself again.

Five minutes later, Maggie bellowed down the hall. "Grace! You can come in now!"

Grace flew to the nursery, putting a hand over her heart in astonishment. "It looks like something out of *Southern Living* magazine!"

Lace drapes hung from the window, highlighting a wallpaper border that had been pasted in the middle of the walls. The paper was decorated with blue trains and rocking horses. Grace gasped, realizing the same border had been hung at the top of the ceiling. On one wall, a mural had been painted of a train chugging through a field where horses grazed. "Tilly," she murmured. "You talented thing. However did you do that?"

"I had lots of good help." Tilly beamed with pride. "I'm so glad you like it."

"Like it! This is a dream come true!" She hugged Tilly's neck, then Cami's, then gave Maggie an especially huge hug. Then she made the rounds of the men, stopping only long enough to try to wipe the paint off of Buzz's nose. "Thank you all so— where's Brant?"

She turned and looked at Maggie. "Is he downstairs?"

Her heart crumbled as Maggie shook her head. "He had to get on home," she explained. "He said he'd call you later."

"Oh," Grace murmured, before smiling brightly for her guests. She was determined to act as if his absence didn't affect her, even if it hurt her beyond words that he wasn't here to see the unveiling of their baby's nursery. "Well, let's pull this bassinet in here, just for starters, so I can get the full effect." She hurried down the hall, wiping a tear that had nothing to do with hormones from her eyes. Rolling the basket into the nursery, where all her friends gathered around to admire it, Grace realized that the baby bumper fabric matched the wallpaper border. She bit her lip, reminding herself that these people had done

an awful lot for her, and that she owed them a happy
face. Who cared if Brant had bailed out on her?

She shouldn't be one bit surprised that he would
kiss and run.

BRANT HATED TO LEAVE Grace without saying goodbye. He would have liked to see the look on her face
when she saw the nursery. As far as he could tell,
the duded-up room was everything a mom could
want for her child. When Grace saw all the love and
thought that had gone into what her friends had done,
Brant had a feeling the woman was going to tear up
and bawl far worse than she had over the bassinet.

He should be there to hold her. Maybe even sneak
in a kiss or two under the guise of concern.

His truck rumbled into the town square, past one
of the four stoplights Fairhaven possessed. As usual,
he scanned the sidewalks looking for faces he recognized. Carpenter's Fine Jewelry was emblazoned
in gold letters above a gold crown on a shop window.
Brant winced. He wasn't quite ready for that, though
it was good to know where Dan had gotten the ring
for Cami. All in all, Brant thought the gentle horse
breeder seemed to adore his little sister. It was a
thought that made it a little easier to give her away.

Dad's giving her away. Brant pulled his mind back
from the reminder, at the same time jerking his gaze
away from Carpenter's window. His eyes lit on Kyle
Macaffee, who was talking to an elderly woman. He
knelt to examine the dog she had on a short, pink
leash even as he appeared to be listening to the old
woman.

Brant didn't slow the truck to wave the way he
might once have. He regretted the words he and Kyle

had spoken to each other. The man was a fine vet, and an honest one. If he couldn't fix what was ailing your livestock, he told you so without false hope. One day, Brant hoped to recharge that business relationship based on mutual trust. He hadn't meant his threat that he'd take his business elsewhere, and he sincerely wished he hadn't said it.

Kyle and Dan were similar men, he realized with a sudden flash of discomfort. Gentle, kind, sensitive to people. He, Brant, was more given to the brisk approach—and if Cami could be believed, some underdeveloped ideas where women were concerned.

That sad notion brought him back around to the most brisk, emotionally underdeveloped, insensitive man he knew: his father. Brant hadn't left Grace's house to go home and take care of the livestock, as he'd said, as much as he had a chore to take care of he was completely dreading.

He could no longer put off calling his folks to tell them they were going to be grandparents—twice.

Chapter Eleven

Forty minutes later, Brant was treated to Elsa Durning's sharp gasp of dismay. "Not you, too, Brant! What is going on with you and Cami?"

Very well that his mother might ask, Brant thought wryly. He hadn't expected his news to be anything less than a shock. "I couldn't tell you, Mother. Bad timing, I guess."

"I...just don't know what to say." She was quiet for a few moments. "Does this have anything to do with us getting a divorce?"

He knew what she was referring to. "No, Mom." He sighed heavily. "I wish I could blame this on someone. Unfortunately I have no one to blame but myself. The laugh's on me, to be honest. I was all set to yell Cami's ears pink for being careless, and then discovered myself in a similar predicament."

"Yes, but Cami's getting married." His mother's voice was perplexed. "And well before the baby's born. Can I expect like news from you?"

He scrubbed his neck sharply. "I don't think so, Mom."

The silence on the line was so long he wondered

if she'd fainted. "Can I ask who the mother of your child is?"

Rolling his eyes at the reaction he knew he was about to receive, he said, "Grace Barclay."

"Grace Barclay!" his mother shrieked. "You…we…son, listen, I don't mean to interfere, but Grace is from a fine family, one we've known for years. You just can't get her in the family way and then not marry her."

"She won't marry me."

"I don't care what you say, Brant, this generation's got to start living up to its responsibilities. This is no roadside trollop you've impregnated like a troublesome mare, this is a girl from a good family."

"Mom, did you hear me? She won't marry me."

He heard a sniff at the other end. "Maybe you haven't asked properly. Brant, it's none of my business, but I doubt you know how to…well, I'm sure you knew well enough how to take care of the, um, part of the relationship that requires the least verbal communication, but talking to a woman is what requires the most finesse. Trust me."

Brant closed his eyes and shook his head. This was a hard conversation to have with his mother. "I've done my best."

"Try harder," she snapped. "You have the future of a baby hanging in the balance. Put your energy into telling that woman what she wants to hear, and do it soon. You're not going to like some other man raising your child, Brant Durning. And if Grace doesn't marry you, she will marry someone, someday."

Cami had said the same thing. A vision of kind Kyle Macaffee patting an old lady's dog loomed in his mind. Brant grimaced, knowing that his mother was speaking from the voice of experience. If he didn't like the fact that his parents had divorced, he would have liked it a lot less if his father had been in Brant's situation and never married her.

"I hope you'll have this remedied by the wedding next weekend, Brant. I'm sorry for the harsh words," she said, her voice softening. "I just hate for you to suffer because of the mistakes your father and I made."

Brant bit his lip, forcing his emotions back. "I have to call Dad and tell him."

She was silent for a long time. "Good luck."

He snorted, his stomach in knots. "Mother," he said quietly, "I don't suppose you have any suggestions?"

They both knew what he was asking. His mother sighed heavily. "I wouldn't like to suggest anything that might make your problem worse, Brant."

"Can't." He couldn't say anymore for the choking sensation in his throat.

"Do you love her, son?"

"I always have. She doesn't believe that, though. With good reason."

"I see." He thought he heard her sniffle again. Then she said, "I'm not a good person to ask for advice."

Brant had to know. "What would have changed your mind? What would have made you stay, Mom?"

She hesitated. "Well, it was much different for me. You and Cami were grown. You didn't need us, anymore."

We did, Mom, he wanted to shout. But he didn't.

"I just needed more, Brant. And your father couldn't give it to me. I couldn't face the thought of all those years ahead of us on that huge ranch with no love in the house. No feeling of companionship." She started crying in earnest. "I hate to say it, but once my mind was made up, there wasn't anything your father could have done to change it. I sincerely hope that's not the position you're in, Brant. What really concerns me, though I mean this in a positive sense, is that you and your father are mirror images in many ways. Just as Cami and I are."

His throat dried out. A few moments later, he said goodbye and hung up, feeling torn, racked. Staring at the phone, Brant wondered how he was going to call his father. Still, he had to do it.

One minute later, he dialed his father's number. "Hello?" a gruff voice said, though the greeting sounded more like a demand.

"It's me, Dad."

"Oh. Hello, Brant."

"Did I catch you at a bad time?"

"No."

The master of the understatement, he thought bitterly. No "Surprised to hear from you," no "How are you doing, son?"

"Haven't heard from you in a while, Dad." He was detouring from what he needed to say, but his throat closed.

"How is everything at the ranch?" Michael Durning asked.

"Fine."

Brant didn't know what else to say, and by the clearing of his father's throat, he knew he was just as uncomfortable. There was nothing to do but get it over with. "Guess you're coming to Cami's wedding."

"Yes."

"Well, I have a small announcement of my own."
Now who was understating? "I...I." He steadied his
voice and started over. "I'm going to be a father."

Lord! It sounded terrible having to say that to his
own father! Brant cringed inside, feeling all at once
as if he were an overactive teenager. He really was
going to be a father—and how in the heck was he
going to keep from messing up what he could hardly
comprehend?

*This is the biggest thing I've ever done in my
whole life,* Brant realized with sudden and overpowering gut instinct. A father was someone a kid looked
up to, respected, trusted—

"You and Cami...are you okay out there?"

"Yes, Dad." Brant sighed and rubbed a weary
hand over his eyes.

"Does your mother know?"

"As of about five minutes ago, yes."

Michael Durning coughed. "So, is there a double
wedding next weekend?"

"No. So far, there isn't going to be another wedding."

"Ah."

Brant waited for about twenty seconds.

"Damned irresponsible of you, son."

"Yeah." Actually, more than his father knew.
"Well, that's all I called to say."

More silence. "I don't suppose I can help you in
any way."

"No." Brant pushed away the bitter thoughts in
his mind. One fought back before he could stop it.

You can tell me how to keep from losing my woman the way you lost Mom. But he didn't say it, the same way he hadn't told his mother that he and Cami had needed her, that they still did, though perhaps in a more adult-to-adult role.

Then he knew. He never said anything that might expose him emotionally. Words that might cost his heart went unsaid.

Shock made him shy away from the truth. He couldn't be like his father.

He just couldn't.

THURSDAY NIGHT before Cami and Dan's rehearsal dinner, Cami was holed up at the Yellowjacket Cafe. Grace couldn't say the bride was having second thoughts; it was more like she was suffering jitters.

"Cami, can I get you a glass of soda?" Grace asked.

The bride-to-be shook her head. "I don't know what I want. I think I want this whole thing to be over."

"I thought you were looking forward to it!" Grace couldn't believe the stalwart Cami she knew was acting this way.

"I am. I want to marry Dan more than anything!" She lowered her voice confidentially, though no one could hear them. Tilly and Maggie were in the kitchen, where Sheriff John was bothering the broadly smiling owner. Buzz and Purvis were glued to their barrel seats, and other than a few customers eating dinner, no one was around who cared to listen to Cami's onset of nerves. "It's just that my folks are coming in tomorrow night. It's got me in a dither, I guess."

Grace frowned. "They're not arriving together, are they?"

"No. Mom's taking a plane in from Florida, and Dad's flying in from his place in Montana. But they'll arrive within an hour of each other at the airport, and Brant and I are going out to pick them up. At least he'll be with me."

Grace cast her eyes toward the table. She'd heard barely a word from Brant since he'd kissed her at the baby shower. He'd called once to see how she was doing, but that was it. His no-show behavior hurt her feelings, though this was exactly the relationship they'd agreed to. Somehow, after they'd kissed, Grace supposed she had begun hoping that…well, that pigs would fly. Nothing really had changed between them, except that they'd given in to the attraction they'd always felt for each other.

"I'm sure everything will go fine," she murmured. "It's your big weekend. Your parents will be on their best behavior."

"I know." Cami sighed, and for the first time, Grace noticed the dark smudges under her eyes. "It's just hard. I mean, I've given Brant the very devil for letting our parents' divorce bother him so much. The truth is, I haven't let myself think too much about it. Taking over the ranch has kept Brant and I so busy, I just didn't allow myself to dwell on it. But they're going to be here in Fairhaven, together again, and I'm expecting a baby…oh, I don't know," she sighed. "It's going to be so awkward."

Grace had been suffering from the same kind of twinges. Spending the weekend around Brant at a marriage ceremony was going to be tough. She reached over to pat Cami's hand. "In three days, you'll be cruising in the Mediterranean. I hope you've chosen appropriate sunbathing wear.''

Cami laughed, some of the fatigue disappearing from her eyes. ''I can't wait for that.'' She nodded her head in the direction of the kitchen.

John had sneaked a hand around Maggie's waist. She moved away swiftly, rapping his hand with a wooden spatula. Grace laughed as he shrugged and walked their way.

''Don't you know Maggie's kitchen is a dangerous place to be, John?''

''I do know it.'' He took a seat at their table. ''Guess I'll take refuge over here with you two.''

''It's a little safer here,'' Cami began. ''Uh-oh. Here comes my brother. Brant! Over here!''

Grace wanted to shrink into her chair. Did Cami have to be so exuberant with her holler to Brant? Her stomach suddenly constricting, she forced a smile to her face.

''Brant Durning! Haven't seen you all week.'' John pulled a chair out for him. ''Thought maybe you were avoiding us.''

''Nah.'' Brant nodded at Grace and his sister. ''I'm still picking wallpaper paste out of my eyelids,'' he groused.

His eyes looked tired and red, as if he was telling the truth, Grace thought. Actually he was wearing the same pensive expression Cami'd had on her face thirty minutes ago.

''So. What's new?'' John asked him.

''Not much. Just catching up with some spring chores. Trying to get the place spruced up some, too. Guests start arriving tomorrow.''

"Yep." John nodded, his eyes lighting as Maggie neared.

"Can I get you something, Brant?"

"A cola and a turkey sandwich. Split it with me?" he asked Grace.

Her heart rate accelerated. "I just ate. Thanks, though."

"You look good."

His comment was the same as if he were looking over one of his steers, Grace warned herself. He hadn't said anything special. She nodded warily in thanks for his compliment but didn't reply.

"Mom just called," Brant told Cami.

"Has she got mother-of-the-bride nerves?" she asked.

"Don't think so. She wanted to remind us that she's bringing Dr. Nelson with her."

Cami's jaw dropped. Grace looked away in embarrassment. Dr. Nelson was Mrs. Durning's new husband, though neither Cami nor Brant ever mentioned him. To them, she was still Elsa Durning.

"Well, that only edges the discomfort level up a notch," Cami commented. "I don't think Dad's going to enjoy this wedding very much."

"None of us are." Brant jerked his eyes up as everyone at the table gasped. "I didn't mean that, Cami! I meant—oh, heck."

John shook his head at him. Brant put his hands up in a warning gesture. "Hey! I'm sorry. I'm glad Cami's getting married. It's all the other stuff that's going along with it that's a pain." To John, he said caustically, "I hope you're taking notes. One day it's gonna be you sitting in the hot seat."

John's eyes darted toward Maggie, who was putting up an order, her dark hands flying competently. "Uh-uh. You'll have to find someone else to feel sorry for you. Maggie knew what I was about before she got involved with me."

"Yeah, well." Brant glanced at Grace. Instantly her heart shrank at the look in his eyes. If she didn't know better, she would think his expression was saying, "So did Grace. And look at the position I'm in now."

Stunned, she sipped at her drink. Was that why Brant had only eked out a cursory phone call to check on her? Had the nursery decorating been more than his bachelor heart could stand? Or had he suddenly realized what she had feared he would all along—that the commitment growing in her belly was more than a wedding ring could make up for?

"I think I'll go on home." She rose from the table, unable to meet Brant's eyes. Nodding to John, Grace gave Cami a quick hug. "Good luck tomorrow night. Call me when you get in from the airport if you want to talk."

She waved to Maggie and Tilly, and said goodnight to Buzz and Purvis as she sailed past them. Once on the sidewalk, Grace hurried toward her house, her feelings hurt and frightened.

"Don't think you'll have to eat that turkey sandwich, Brant," Cami said mildly as Tilly put the plate in front of him. "You can't possibly be hungry after putting your foot in your mouth."

"What'd I say?" Grace's swift exit had alerted him that something had gone awry, but he hadn't even spoken to her! In fact, he was trying very hard not to say anything to make matters worse between them. He'd spent most of the week trying to figure out what he should say to Grace. He loved her; she knew that. She just didn't believe he loved her for her. How was a man supposed to get around that roadblock?

"I don't know if it's what you say so much as what you don't say." Cami sighed, reaching over to grab the half of the sandwich he'd offered Grace. "And when you talk about my wedding, the look on your face spells panic."

"Well, damn it! I am!"

"I know." She bit into the sandwich. "I am, too. But Grace read it as something else, I think. What do you think, John?"

"I think it's time for Maggie to close up shop," he said, watching the owner of the Yellowjacket Cafe with a gleam in his dark eyes. "She's supposed to cut my hair tonight."

Cami stared at him, then at Brant. "You know, you two are frighteningly similar."

"What's that supposed to mean?" Brant demanded.

His sister shook her head, a maddeningly knowing look on her face. "You both are suffering from macho, barbaric personalities." She ignored the heated denials from both men. "In your case, John, you have a little more time to work out the kinks. But, brother, if I was you, I'd at least put a quarter in the phone and call Grace to whisper good-night in her ear. I'm thinking it's going to be an awfully long weekend for you if you don't."

Cami got up and left the table abruptly. Brant stared after her.

"What was that all about?" John wanted to know.

"I'm not sure," Brant murmured. "Ever since my

little sister got pregnant, she's been an irritating fountain of knowledge.''

"Mmm," John grunted. "Bad side effect."

"I don't know," Brant said thoughtfully. "What's irritating about it is that so far, she's been right on the bull's-eye." He bit the inside of his jaw before getting to his feet. "John, I'm going to have to call it a night."

The sheriff sighed. "You losing a quarter or throwing gravel tonight?"

"I think I'll try ringing the doorbell this time." Brant shook his head. "Though if Cami's right, Grace isn't going to open the door."

"Well, don't make me have to come after you for disturbing the peace."

Brant waved John's comment off and beat a hasty retreat. He'd spent all week grappling with the conversation between him and his father, and trying to figure out a way to convince Grace that he wasn't in this thing simply because of the baby.

Ringing the doorbell at Grace's house, he waited impatiently on the porch. There was no answer, and belatedly Brant realized there were no lights on inside. That had to mean she was at her shop. Striding back up the sidewalk, he headed toward the Wedding Wonderland. If he'd been smart, he would have checked there first, since it was right across the street from the Yellowjacket.

Peering through the window, he saw a light on inside a stockroom. He tried the door handle, but it barely moved. Pushing at it more firmly, Brant felt the door move inward.

Instantly the security system wailed its announcement of a break-in at the Wedding Wonderland.

Chapter Twelve

Brant practically jumped out of his skin. Reflexively he jerked the door shut, but the alarm continued shrieking. Glancing over his shoulder, he saw the regulars peering out the window at him. He could practically hear the laughter.

The door gave way in front of him. "What in the world are you doing, Brant?" Grace demanded. She looked as if he'd scared her badly. That was the last thing he'd wanted to do.

She touched some numbers into the alarm panel in a box by the door. Welcome—yet strained—silence fell between them.

He needed to explain his behavior. "I was going to—"

Behind him, he heard Sheriff John's lazy whistling. Brant cringed.

"I see you got Grace to open the door, Brant," he called. "Maybe next time the Fairhaven High School band could help you get Grace's attention. The police don't like having to come out for false alarms."

"I'll keep that in mind, John." In the Cafe window, Brant could see Cami shaking her head at him. He felt a momentary strike of annoyance that his private life was always so public in this town. But wasn't that what Grace had tried to explain to him? She'd said he was so worried about what other people thought that he didn't show any expression at all. She'd said these people were their friends. Glancing back at Grace, he felt a larger fear that he might have turned into the cardboard man that his father was.

"I'm sorry, Grace," he said, throwing caution to the wind. "I stopped by your house, but you weren't there. I took a chance that you were here."

"I'm catching up on some book work." Her eyes were huge in her face, the lines around them tired, from what he could see in the light of the lamp hanging above the door.

"I didn't mean to frighten you out of your wits." He paused, glancing down at her stomach. "Hope the little guy's okay."

A tiny smile floated onto her face. "It didn't disturb him in the least."

His boy was brave! Brant liked that idea. "Grace, the reason I was trying to find you is because I think I owe you an apology."

Her gaze dropped, but at least she didn't slam the door shut. He forged ahead. "I'm not sure what I said in the Cafe, but what is clear to me is that somehow I upset you. Grace, that's the last thing I want to do." He reached out to smooth a curl behind her ear, and Grace's eyes jumped up to meet his.

"It's okay," she said softly.

"No, it's not. Tell me what I said."

She shrugged. "You didn't say anything. I think...I think I feel that you resent me for this."

She touched her stomach, which Brant couldn't help noticing seemed larger than when he'd seen her last Sunday. He eyed it curiously. "I don't resent you at all. I just don't know how to make it right."

"What do you mean?" The overhead lamp sent a soft glow onto her face, and Brant thought she'd never looked so beautiful, so alluring.

"I'm not sure myself, but I'm going to give it a try." One last backward glance over his shoulder sent the regulars skittering from the window. "You're beautiful, babe. I know I never said it while we were dating, but you were the only woman I could ever spend an entire night thinking about. I don't mean just the hours before I went to bed. I mean the entire night. I spent months trying to figure out how I was going to…to, well, get you to let me make love to you."

Grace's mouth dropped open. "What is the matter with you?"

He frowned. "What do you mean?"

"You sound like you've got an extra dose of pregnancy hormones or something! I've never heard you so…emotional."

Brant decided to take Grace's astonishment in stride. What was she supposed to think, with him doing a one-hundred-eighty-degree turn on her? "I've had a lot of time to think in the last week," he began, not able to tell her that talking to his father had convinced him that he didn't want to always keep his feelings under tight rein. "I've had a lot of time to think about us. I want you to know that I'm sorry for everything."

Grace hesitated before shaking her head. "I'm not."

"No, I don't mean that." Anxiety made him rush his next words. "I wish I hadn't been so paranoid about loving you, Grace. That's all I'm going to say right now, because I don't want to rush you. I want you to have time to think about what I've said. But think about this—I spent the last three months trying to get you out of my system. I couldn't.''

He dropped a last kiss on Grace's lips. "Can I walk you home, or do you still have work to finish?"

"I have about another hour's worth." The confusion in Grace's eyes told Brant that what he'd said was long overdue.

"Will you be careful walking home?" he asked her. "I worry about you."

"John and Maggie will walk me home, after she finishes closing up the Cafe." She stepped back inside the door. "Thank you for coming by, Brant."

He jammed the Western hat he was carrying back on his head. "You think about what I've said."

"I will. Good night."

She closed the door softly, and Brant headed toward his truck. Somehow, he felt as if he'd made headway. In the next couple of months, he ought to be able to manage some more.

Maybe he could even get Grace to the altar before his son was born.

GRACE HELD WONDERING fingertips over her mouth as she covertly watched Brant through the lace curtains. What had gotten into him? All this sudden rush to spill his heart out to her had something to do with his parents' arrival tomorrow night, Grace felt sure. She'd never seen Cami as upset as she was, either. One minute Cami had been a blushing bride-to-be; tonight she was more nervous than a mare around a stallion.

She backed away from the window, her hand falling to caress her stomach. Maybe his folks had put the pressure on him to marry her. Grace shook her head at that notion. Nobody pressured Brant Durning to do anything. He and Cami were alike in few ways, but they did share that trait.

Could it be that he actually wanted to marry her? She thought about the regretful look she'd seen in his eyes as John was proclaiming his intention to stay single. Possibly she'd misread what she'd seen in his eyes.

Sighing, Grace walked to stand in front of a three-way mirror. Her stomach protruded without any lack of restraint now. She decided to wait until after this weekend was over—and Cami and Brant's parents had gone home—to ponder his words. In all likelihood, everyone was simply suffering from an advanced case of wedding overexcitement. She didn't want to read too much into Brant's words in case he had been propelled into them by something other than a real desire to marry her.

All the same, Grace couldn't help thinking as she eyed her stomach in the three-way mirror that she hoped Brant meant what he was saying. Time was running out.

"SOMETHING'S WRONG," Maggie proclaimed darkly. "I don't know what, but it is." She reached over and smacked John's roving hand with the wooden spatula for the eighth time that evening.

"Ouch!" he cried. "Maggie, that hurt!"

She never smacked him hard enough to cause him pain, but she was plain out of patience tonight. "Quit trying to pat my behind, John. I've got a lot on my mind.''

Comforting fingers massaged into her shoulders. ''I'm sorry, Maggie. Guess I was thinking about getting you alone.''

''I know. But I'm too upset.'' Maggie sighed and turned to face John. ''Did you get an eyeful of Grace's stomach tonight?''

He rubbed his face thoughtfully. ''I reckon it looked like she's growing a bun in her oven, same as she has for a few months now.''

Tilly glanced up from where she was cleaning off the counter. It was past closing time, and they were doing the nightly cleanup. They were alone, the three of them. Even Buzz and Purvis got shooed off when the doors locked. ''What's going around in that mind of yours, Maggie?''

''It's something I can hardly explain.'' She attacked a dirty pot with gusto. ''For the last couple of weeks, I've been having this notion that Grace is bigger than she oughta be. Now, I know she had a sonogram, and those things are s'posed to be reliable, but my gut's telling me an error's been rung up somewhere.''

Tilly gasped. ''Don't you think Brig Delancey knows what he's about?''

Maggie nodded. ''That's what's bothering me. Now, if it was the old doc, I mighta been more worried, 'cause Lord knows he was getting feeble. But Doc Brig knows his stuff.'' She tossed down the pot and picked up another, scrubbing at the caked beans around the rim. ''And I know that Grace goes regularly for her prenatal checkups. So she's getting measured, and weighed...I know there ain't no way of what I'm thinking to be right, but all the same, something's not right.''

John scratched his head. ''Mistakes are made all the time with those sonograms. Could be the due date was miscalculated?''

''Could be, but Doc Brig's seen her since then, so he would know by her measurements if she wasn't on track.'' Maggie shook her head, completely puzzled. ''What do I know anyway? I ain't a doctor.''

''No, but if you're worrying, there's probably a reason,'' John said, his statement borne out of knowing Maggie Mason for years.

''I was worried enough to rush decorating that nursery.''

Tilly turned. ''Is that why you got all fired-up to do that? You said something about it being cooler in May, and a bunch of other nonsense, but I just figured you were in the mood to decorate.''

''No.'' Maggie shook her head decisively. ''Either Grace Barclay is cooking twins, or she's carrying the biggest baby known to man, or—'' She sighed heavily, knowing no good could come of her next suggestion. ''Or Grace is further along than she knows.''

''How far?''

Maggie squinted toward the Wedding Wonderland. ''I left my crystal ball at home, but judging by the way she's filled out in the last week, and dropped in the middle, too, I'd say we're looking at a run to the hospital in a couple of weeks.''

''Weeks!'' Tilly dropped her sponge. ''Do you think you better mention to Grace what you're thinking? She might need to make another trip in to see

Dr. Delancey. She hasn't had time to go to breast-feeding classes, or coaching classes, or anything!''

Maggie raised her brows at John in question. He held up his hands. ''Don't ask me. We all agreed when Brant came back into town that the less that got said about their situation, the better they'd probably both be. We've kept our interfering to a minimum so far, and nature seems to be taking its course.''

The three of them stared at each other for a moment. '''Course, if you're honestly having misgivings, Maggie, and I've known you too long to think you're just whistling Dixie, somebody might at least mention it to her. She's going to need more than paint and wallpaper if that baby's gonna put in an appearance soon.''

Maggie bit her lip. ''Go get her, John.''

He nodded once, considering, then left the Cafe. A moment later, he'd returned with Grace.

She sank gratefully into a chair. ''I was ready to call it a night,'' she said, putting her feet out in front of her. ''I've got all this energy during the day, but tonight, I'm unusually tired.''

Maggie was eyeing her curiously. Grace raised her brows. ''What?''

Maggie came over to sit across the table from her. Tilly and John grabbed a seat as well. He reached over and lit the candle with his lighter, and the four of them sat in silence watching until the flame caught.

''I don't know how to say what's on my mind, Grace,'' Maggie began. ''I sure don't want to upset you. But I—we were wondering when the last time you saw Dr. Delancey was.''

Grace looked around the table at each of them. "I'm seeing him next week. Why?"

"Well, I don't exactly know."

Maggie's gaze skimmed her stomach, which just rose over the top of the table. Grace sat a little straighter, so the roundness was a little more hidden.

"You have discussed your due date with Doc Brig, right? It wasn't a date you arbitrarily selected based on the last cycle you had?" Maggie watched her closely.

"Where are all these questions leading, Maggie?" Grace suddenly felt nervous. "I've discussed everything with Dr. Delancey. You know I listen closely to whatever he has to say."

"Hmm." Maggie leaned back in the chair. "You've changed in the last few weeks, Grace. There isn't any chance—" She broke off her words. "I don't want to worry you, honey, but you sure don't look like you've got two more months left in you."

Grace clasped her fingers into her skirt to keep them from trembling. "I—I don't know what to say. I'll mention it to Dr. Delancey when I see him." She jumped up from the table, prepared to flee, but John's hand shot out, capturing her wrist.

"I'll walk you home, Grace, if you're of a mind to go." Gently he pulled her down into the seat. "'Course, I gotta tell you something else. I've known Miss Maggie a long time, and ain't many times I've known her to be wrong about something. We're not trying to upset you. We're worried about you."

"I know you are." Grace sank into the chair, braving a glance around the table at her friends. The candlelight showed the concern in their eyes, and she was truly ashamed. "I'm sorry," she whispered. "I couldn't tell you the truth. I couldn't tell anyone the truth."

"You mean...you mean I'm right? You are due sooner than you said you were?" Maggie looked shocked.

"Yes." Grace couldn't meet her eyes. "We'll probably have a Brant Durning, Junior, in a couple of weeks."

"Oh, Grace!" Maggie and Tilly jumped up to come around the table and throw their arms around her. "Why didn't you tell us?" Maggie demanded.

Tears began flowing down her cheeks. "I didn't want anyone to know! And after Brant came back, I didn't want him to feel pressured to marry me. I wanted him to have as much time as possible to think about being a father." She began sobbing in earnest, unable to help the tears that wouldn't stop.

Her back was being rubbed soothingly, but Grace couldn't be soothed. "The truth is, I knew I was pregnant when I mentioned marriage to Brant back in the fall. I told you I found out after he left, but I was already at the end of the first trimester when we broke up. I spent three months hiding out, hiding my stomach, hoping he was going to change his mind and come back to me. But then, he flat-out left Fairhaven, and there I was, six months pregnant."

Grace blew into the tissue Maggie had pressed into her hand. "Of course, Dr. Delancey wasn't going to give me away. I should have told you," she said with an apologetic glance around at her friends, "but I guess I was trying to put off the inevitable as long as possible."

"You sure had us fooled," Maggie said, her voice awed. "I guess it's because you're tall that you kept it hidden so well, but you surely only started looking full of baby this month." She blew out a heavy breath. "Grace Barclay, we don't have time for those coaching classes!"

She smiled ruefully. "I figured they weren't going to tell us anything you didn't already know, Maggie." Reaching out, she touched her fingers to her friend's. "I don't think they can teach you anything."

Maggie straightened, nodding with pride. "We'll do fine, Grace." Her eyes suddenly filled with tears, too. Tilly sniffled, and John glanced away. "Great day in the morning," Maggie said, her voice breaking, "that baby's already in the home stretch, John! We're gonna have us a baby before we know it!"

They all laughed, and then shed a few more happy tears. Grace looked around at her friends who so obviously shared her elation. It felt wonderful to get her secret off her chest.

Almost off her chest. Sooner or later, she was going to have to tell Brant the truth. This was not the weekend to disrupt what little equilibrium he had left.

"You just gonna let that little baby make a surprise announcement on the daddy," Tilly asked, putting a name to the thoughts in Grace's head, "or are you going to give him some advance warning?"

Grace hesitated the slightest second. "If you will all keep my secret a while longer, I promise I'll tell him right after Cami's wedding."

"Right after, as in once the rice is thrown?" Maggie demanded suspiciously. "Or right after, as in sometime in the next two weeks, and preferably after John and I've run you up to the hospital?''

"Right after his parents have gone home, I'll tell him." Grace tried to control the sudden racing of her heart. "I promise."

Chapter Thirteen

Brant could honestly say he'd never been more nervous in his life as he waited for his parents' planes to arrive. Beside him, Cami was silent, which glaringly announced her own nervousness. He couldn't remember the last time his sister hadn't been boiling over with delirious excitement since he'd returned home.

"Brant! Cami! Yoo-hoo!" a cheery voice called.

His mother ran toward them, bags and packages askew, and followed by a tall, distinguished man. She threw her arms around Cami first, giving her a tight squeeze. "Cami! I can't believe my little girl is getting married." She pulled away briefly, staring at her stomach before pulling her close again. "You look wonderful!"

Brant felt his mother's hand reach out to pull him into the embrace. He went willingly into the whimsical circle of his mother's love and perfumed scent and exuberance. She was like Cami that way, a delightful whirlwind bringing pleasure to everyone around her. Brant tried not to think about the man standing behind her, patiently waiting for the awkward mumblings of welcome that he had probably

come to expect from the Durning clan. A part of him
had to admire that Dr. Nelson would go through this
for his mother's sake. Dr. Nelson, fossil finder and
archaeological authority, who took his mother to fascinating places in his hunt for the history of life,
Brant thought sourly.

He forced himself to break away from his mother
to face Dr. Nelson. Putting out a hand, he said,
"Welcome. Let me help you with some of those
packages Mother's loaded you down with."

The man smiled, his expression appreciative at
Brant's overture, but not overeager. Cami remembered her manners at the same time.

"Thank you for coming, Dr. Nelson," she said,
her voice only slightly cool for the Cami Brant knew.
"I...I—"

Brant was horrified when his sister burst into tears.
Cami never cried!

"I'm sorry," she moaned, "I don't know why I'm
crying."

"Maybe I shouldn't have come," kindly Dr. Nelson said, his voice distressed.

"No, no!" Cami waved her hand and scrubbed her
eyes. "I honestly don't know what's come over me."

"Ah." Brant had experience with this. Cami was
having a tomato moment extraordinaire. Thanks to
Grace, he knew what he was dealing with. He pulled
his sister to him to support her, and jerked his head
in the direction of the luggage carousel. "Dr. Nelson,
if you'll get your suitcases, Cami and I'll get the
car."

"Fine, fine, Brant. Call me Bob, if you would.
Hate to stand on formality," he said, glancing at

Cami in some alarm. "Can I get you a glass of water?"

"Cami, are you all right?" Elsa Durning Nelson asked.

"She's fine." Brant pulled his sister to the sliding doors with him. "We'll be right back with the car."

Once in the bright sunshine, Cami pulled away and dabbed at her nose. "I wish I hadn't done that!"

"It doesn't matter," Brant said curtly, watching the traffic before they stepped out. "If you hadn't, I probably would have."

"Really?" Cami stared up at him in astonishment.

"Hell, yeah. I feel like bawling like a baby. It doesn't help that Bob is so nice, either. I'd like to hate him. But all I can do is…face the facts, Cam. Mom's happier than I've ever seen her."

His sister halted right in the middle of the street. Brant tugged her to safety. "You're right. You know, you're really right, Brant. For once."

Airplanes whined overhead, and taxis whizzed past impatiently. He shrugged at her teasing. "Miracles happen, I guess."

"I thought I was the smart one in the family." Cami's nose was red and her burnished curls looked forlorn somehow. Brant reached out to give her a swift hug.

"I might have had some catching up to do, but I'm getting there." Of course, he needed a lot more coaching.

"Well, the prospect of being a father certainly seems to agree with you."

Brant took off in the direction of the car. "Maybe."

It wasn't that, but he wasn't going to tell his wiseacre sister all his secrets. He had a few more months to think about being a father. That wasn't what was shifting his thought process into high, enlightened gear.

It was trying to figure out how to get his reluctant woman to the altar that was forcing him to think on a higher plane. He had a goal. He wanted a "yes" out of Grace Barclay—and he wanted it soon.

No baby of his was going to think that his father hadn't wanted him.

WHEN HE AND CAMI had pulled the car around, Brant was dismayed to see his father waiting on the sidewalk with Bob and Elsa. "Oh, boy, oh, boy," he said sarcastically to Cami. "Isn't this going to be a fun ride home."

He got out of the car, walking to shake hands briskly with his father. Cami managed a hug and a fast kiss on the cheek for him.

"Plane get in early, Dad?" he asked. If his mother had looked dazzlingly happy ten minutes ago, she looked downright unhappy right now.

"Actually it was right on schedule. I must have gotten the flight times mixed up."

"Oh." Brant tossed his father's suitcase into the trunk. That wasn't too hard to envision happening. Elsa Durning had been the anchor that held his father in place for nearly thirty years.

Silently they all got into the car, Michael Durning up front beside Brant who was driving. Bob, Elsa and Cami squeezed in the back. Brant ground his jaw as he maneuvered the car into traffic.

Grace was going to marry him, he decided obstinately, and when she said yes, she wasn't ever going to go flying off with some archaeological fossil finder who could give her what he couldn't. Or some kind-hearted veterinarian, either.

Brant might have been slow in catching up, but he was about to make up for lost time.

GRACE DOUBLED OVER at the sudden pain in her stomach. The baby's kicks had grown more insistent in the past few weeks, making it much harder to ignore them. She'd been beset by aches and pains that she'd never dreamed pregnancy would bring her. Lying on the bed, Grace told herself all she had to do was get through the rehearsal dinner tonight, then the wedding tomorrow night. Then she could put on sweatpants and big tops and be comfortable for the next two weeks. Her sister, Hope, a high school teacher, was coming into town to oversee the shop for her, and that was the biggest relief of all to Grace. Now that it was the end of May, Hope was on break, and was planning to spend the summer helping Grace with the new baby.

Sighing, she couldn't help thinking that she was lucky to have all the help she was getting. She was better prepared for single motherhood than most women in her position might be. The most surprising event was Brant trying harder to woo her, which was nice, in a way.

In another way, it was unsettling. She'd seen the determined glint in his eye, saw it blossom and take shape last night when he'd set off the alarm at the Wedding Wonderland. When he found out that he was going to be a father a lot sooner than he expected, Grace had no doubts that Brant was going to insist on getting married immediately. Well, first he was going to be mad as the dickens that she'd deceived him. But as soon as that passed, Brant's let's-get-this-thing-done personality was going to dictate a quick solution.

Grace meant to stick to her guns on this matter. She wasn't going to marry a man who had run out the door at the first wind of permanent commitment. She'd spent too many months alone, frightened into planning for a future for her and her baby. That future hadn't included Brant, and she saw no reason to change the picture, when she had everything so well organized. Brant was only putting forth this extreme effort toward marriage because of the baby—as his grudging marriage proposal in the hotel in New York attested.

For days, she'd watched Cami and Brant suffer over having to see their parents in the same house but no longer together. Grace wasn't going to give her baby the same future. After all, Brant had picked up and left her once.

Who was to say he wouldn't do it again?

THE REHEARSAL DINNER was true to its name, Brant thought grimly, sitting at a table in a fancy restaurant in Fairhaven. They were rehearsing parts they all were going to play at the altar tomorrow night. He felt sorry for Cami and Dan. They were supposed to be the happy bridal couple, and he didn't think he'd ever seen more miserable people.

The rehearsal itself had gone just fine, perhaps because the minister and a few support staff from the church were looking on. But now he, Grace—as Cami's maid of honor—his parents and the bridal couple were alone, trying to figure out what to say to each other. Dr. Nelson of the exquisite manners wouldn't intrude on a private family matter and had taken himself off to Glen Rose to see the dinosaur footprints. Despite his absence, nobody was comfortable.

Though Grace looked beautiful, she also looked heavy with her pregnancy. Brant wondered how she could get much bigger than she was, and felt a momentary surge of pride in his son. Obviously the boy was going to be a linebacker! The pride somewhat deteriorated when he realized his mother was staring at Grace, though trying not to be too obvious about the direction of her gaze. Cami was nowhere near showing.

"Is your food all right, Grace?" his mother asked. She had been in the process of making overly polite conversation with Cami's fiancé, but had taken a moment out to shoot a worried look Grace's way.

"It's delicious, thank you." Grace smiled, but it wasn't her usual bright smile. Brant felt a moment's worry that she was overtired. After this weekend was over, he would insist that she get plenty of rest. Under the table, he reached over to rub the top of her leg soothingly. Grace started, before actually seeming to draw some comfort from his gesture.

"Are you all right?" he leaned over to whisper in her ear.

"I'm fine. Don't worry about me," she whispered back.

He patted her leg, before glancing up to catch his father's stern eye on him. "More bread, Dad?" he asked, passing the rolls to that end of the table.

"No, thank you." He hesitated for a moment.

''Well, Dan, I guess you and Cami are looking forward to your honeymoon.''

''Yes, we are.''

Dan appeared to be blushing, and Brant felt momentary pity for him. No doubt he was remembering the hell Brant had raised on him when he'd discovered Cami was pregnant, and assumed any moment Michael Durning was going to blow. Brant snorted to himself. If his dad blew at anyone, he'd be shocked.

''Well, I must say, this isn't the way I envisioned things happening for my children,'' Elsa said brightly. ''Two grandchildren, for heaven's sake. I'll have to join a frequent flyer program so I can see my grandbabies often.''

Nobody had much to say to that. Brant thought that was probably the quickest rehearsal dinner anyone had ever had in history. They vacated the restaurant, and thirty minutes later, he was putting Grace into her truck.

''I wish you had let me pick you up,'' he said. ''Will you at least let me drive you to the church tomorrow, and then up to the Double D? You're going to have a lot to carry, Grace, with your dress and all.''

''I'll be all right.'' She started the engine.

''Grace, I'm going to pick you up tomorrow night,'' he stated, his tone no-nonsense. ''If you don't need me, I sure as hell need you. This weekend is just about the biggest fiasco I've ever seen.''

''I know.'' She paused to look up at him. ''Poor Cami!''

''Maybe the champagne tomorrow night will

loosen everyone up. Besides, there'll be so many guests at the D that it'll feel less awkward.''

"I hope you're right." Grace's expression softened. "Cami's going to be such a beautiful bride."

"Yeah." Grace would be one, too. He planned on telling her that very thing tomorrow night. Tonight had not been the night to ask her to become a limb on his family tree. After the wedding, he was sure his folks would unbend enough to appear less intimidating to Grace.

"Well, good night, Brant." Grace smiled, but he was once again struck by how tired she looked.

"Are you sure this wedding isn't too much? I don't want you shaking anything loose too soon," he tried to tease. It fell flat, by the look on Grace's face. "Tilly could stand in for you, you know, if you're not feeling up to it."

"We'll only be throwing birdseed tomorrow night, and I can get plenty of rest after that. Besides, I've let all the seams out of my maid of honor dress. Tilly couldn't fit into it unless there were two of her." She sighed heavily. "I haven't been sleeping well is all."

He leaned through the truck window and gave her a lingering kiss on the mouth before she could pull away. "Sleep better tonight, Grace Barclay. I may need you to hold me up at the altar."

"Not sleeping well, either?"

"I don't think I will tonight. We've got to take Dan out for his bachelor party."

"Oh! I'd forgotten about that." The look on Grace's face turned distinctly unhappy, but Brant wasn't sure why.

He reached out to run a hand along her cheek, and

one finger along the tiny freckles there. "Did I tell you that you look beautiful tonight?"

"No, but you don't have to tell me every single night, Brant."

Still, Grace perked up a little. Brant gave her a devilish grin. "I noticed my boy's pushing you out of shape quite a bit. You don't let him keep you up all night playing tag, okay?"

Her gaze slid away from his. "I won't."

"Well, I'll pick you up tomorrow afternoon, about five?"

She nodded slowly. "I'll be ready."

Brant stepped away from the truck so she could drive away. He watched the taillights disappear in the dark, the strangest notion hitting him that Grace hadn't once smiled, or laughed, all evening.

Maybe it was worth putting a call in to Dr. Delancey. Then again, the doctor wouldn't discuss Grace's pregnancy with him, particularly as they weren't married.

That was a situation that could be remedied sooner than later.

WHEN BRANT RETURNED to the Double D to meet Dan, who insisted on dropping Cami off at home, he found a pair of unsmiling parents waiting for him in the den.

"We'd like to have a word with you, Brant." His father's voice was stern. His mother's posture was stiff.

"Sure." Brant threw himself into a chair across from them. "What's up?"

"What's up with you?" his mother demanded tartly. "When are you going to marry Grace?"

"As soon as she'll have me." Brant shrugged at them. "I already told you that on the phone."

"You didn't tell us you were running out of time!" his mother nearly shrieked. "You said she was pregnant. You didn't say she was due any minute!"

"Now, wait a second." Brant held up a conciliatory hand. "Grace isn't due for another couple of months. I think her due date's in August. I still have time to change her mind."

His father shook his head. Elsa stared at him. "Son, you have lived on a ranch too long not to know a female who's in the extremely advanced stages of pregnancy."

Something discomforting began edging into Brant's brain. He gave his mother a suspicious, sideways glance. "Are we calling six or seven months advanced?"

"No," she snapped. "We're calling a full nine months of gestation and about-to-deliver-any-day-now advanced."

"Mom, you're just surprised. Grace has only filled out in the last week. She didn't look like that a few days ago."

Elsa got up and began pacing the room at breakneck speed. "I think you need to have a long heart-to-heart with Grace. Someone's misread their calendar—or someone isn't telling every detail of the story. But if she gets through the wedding tomorrow night, it'll be a miracle."

"I think it's just a big baby," Brant said. "I swear, she just popped out this week."

His father had been silent up till now. "Brant, listen to your mother. She was a nurse for most of her life.''

"I am listening! I can only tell you what I know." He slammed his palm on his knee in disgust. "I have to drive Dan into Dallas for his bachelor party now. Will you feel better if I tell you I had planned on asking Grace to marry me tomorrow night?"

"I thought you said you already had, and that she'd turned you down."

"Yeah, well." Brant's collar got warm. "I think I need to ask her again."

"Well, it might make us feel better, son." His father looked out a window. "Your mother doesn't think there's a whole lot of time left for you to convince Grace that you're suitable husband material."

He appreciated their concern. Yet, he resented it as well. Of all people to be lecturing him on a dash to the altar! "I've got it under control." He gave Elsa a kiss, and his father a brief nod. "Good night, Mother. Father."

"Oh, dear," Elsa moaned as Brant left the room. "This is the kind of predicament I can envision Cami in. But she's been so levelheaded about her situation, while my son is out in left field."

Michael didn't reply. The two of them sat in the den, among the possessions that used to be theirs, until they heard Dan and Brant run down the stairs. Cami shouted something out the upstairs window at the departing men, evoking much laughter.

"Elsa." Michael stood, and she stared at her ex-husband with raised brows. "Sooner or later, Brant will work this out. He may be his father's son, and a bit on the reticent side, but he is also your son, which means that if Grace Barclay thinks she's going to be a single mother forever, she is underestimating Brant. He will love his child with such ferocity that Grace will know she is loved, by the very fact that Brant's heart will never, ever belong to anyone else. I watched you over the years love your children that way, and I think it always frightened me that you could love so much. I know now what a gift that kind of love is. Brant and Cami will have that same love for their spouses, and their children. Tomorrow night, I can leave this house happy, because I know that your legacy is firmly ingrained in those kids.''

Elsa's eyes filled with tears. ''That's the sweetest thing you've ever said to me.''

He nodded, turning to leave the room. ''I have no doubt of that. Losing what you love is a hard way to learn that you should have been more caring of that love all along.''

Elsa stared out the window for a long time after her ex-husband left to go to the hotel where he was staying. She hoped Brant knew what he was doing. Grace hadn't looked at him more than twice all night—and that couldn't bode well for Brant.

Michael might think Brant was a lot like her, but he contained plenty of Michael's traits. If Brant had spent nine months and more giving Grace the cool side of his heart, she didn't think Grace would be too easily convinced to become Mrs. Brant Durning. Michael had spoken his heart far too long after their relationship was over for it to have changed anything for Elsa. She could only pray Grace still wanted Brant.

GRACE TRIED NOT TO THINK about the bachelor party very much. It was just so hard to know that Brant would be looking at a bunch of skinny, dancing women—no doubt minus pertinent pieces of their clothing—while she looked like a dirigible had taken up residence inside her!

She got into bed, telling herself she needed to sleep well for tomorrow. Her conscience would be a lot lighter after she told Brant the truth, even though she knew what his reaction would be. It would be easier to handle Brant in marriage overdrive than continuing to keep this secret. She closed her eyes, almost looking forward to the next twenty-four hours.

For Cami's sake, she hoped the wedding would be a dream come true.

Chapter Fourteen

As Dan's best man, Brant stood at the altar, his gaze moving over Cami's face, and then Grace's. Whatever had been bothering Grace last night appeared to have dissipated. She looked soft and lovely in a pink dress. It was long and beaded, and had a short jacket over it, which for some reason, did an excellent job of concealing her pregnancy. The wedding in the chapel was a private family affair, and Brant couldn't help being glad about that for Grace's sake. Though about twenty-five people were in the chapel, he felt as if the situation was less awkward for Grace this way. By the glow on Cami's and Dan's faces, he suspected they enjoyed saying their vows with only their family and closest friends surrounding them.

Grace took Cami's bouquet from her, so that Dan could slide the ring on her finger. Brant's heart swelled with pride as he watched. His little sister had chosen a fine man to be her husband. Brant hoped that any lingering doubt Dan might have had about his welcome into the family had been dispelled last night at the bachelor party. Though he hadn't been exactly slobbering drunk, Brant had gotten loose enough to apologize for his shotgun approach to making certain Dan intended to marry his sister. He thought Dan had received the apology very well.

After the bachelor party, Brant had slowly driven home, lost in his thoughts. In the lonely, dark streets of Fairhaven, he'd stopped his truck in front of Carpenter's Jewelry Store, his gaze tired but focused. After a moment, he'd circled back around the square, past the Wedding Wonderland, to Grace's house. He'd let his truck idle a moment as he stared up at her darkened windows. Everything had been quiet, and he'd hoped she was getting plenty of rest.

The minister's voice jerked him out of his reverie. With a start, he realized the couple had just been announced as husband and wife. Cami and Dan turned, so Grace bent to straighten the train as the bridal couple walked back up the aisle. Brant winced. The sight of Grace bending over that way looked painful. Gently he took her arm and helped her up before escorting her behind Cami and Dan.

And then it was over. Brant breathed a deep sigh of relief out in the May twilight. Well-wishers thronged around Cami and Dan. Somebody gave Brant a good pounding between his shoulder blades.

"Hey!" Sheriff John exclaimed. "Your feet didn't catch on fire at the altar, Brant! That has to be a good sign."

"Shut up, John," Brant groused. "If I was you, I'd be careful about what I was dishing out. One of these days, you might find yourself in a monkey suit like this and listening to the organ-grinder."

"Uh-uh." He gave Brant a sly nudge. "I did see you giving Grace the look-see a bunch. Maybe going through a marriage ceremony'll get her warmed up for one of her own."

Brant shifted his gaze over to where Grace was being helped into a waiting limo. "Hey, there goes my ride." He pulled at the stiff collar once before thumping John on the back. "You're going to be my best man, John, when I get Grace up there. If anybody needs a warming up, it's you." He pointed a good-natured finger at the sheriff before he jogged to the limo and jumped in next to Grace.

"Hey, gorgeous," he said.

She laughed outright. "Oh, Brant. Don't lay it on so thick."

"I meant it. Have we got this ride all to ourselves?" He gave her a meaningful look. "'Cause if we do, I've got a good mind to give the limo driver something to listen to." Before Grace could react, he blew disgusting, noisy raspberries against her neck.

"Ugh!" She playfully pushed Brant away. "You are in way too good a mood, Brant. What did you get into last night?"

"A little too much beer and nothing else." He leaned his head against the seat, eyeing the partition between them and the driver. "Would you believe I'm getting old? Dan holds more beer than I do."

"Yuck. That's not a product of being old. That's a typical reaction to a man who's getting married in twenty-four hours. They're looking for a comatose state so they can endure the fact that they're actually saying a willing 'yes' to lifelong imprisonment."

The smile slid right off Brant's face as he turned to look at her. "Grace, I wouldn't need a comatose state."

She stared at him before dropping her eyelashes to hide her thoughts. The seat across from them was suddenly filled with yards of white satin and laughing bridal couple.

"We're going to have to ride up to the ranch with you two," Cami informed them. "Sorry, but the wedding limo has broken down. Is that bad luck?"

Grace shook her head. "I think the only bad luck that affects a wedding day is if the groom doesn't show up for the ceremony."

Instinctively her gaze met Brant's startled one.

Dan banged on the glass partition. "Get this buggy hauling, driver! I got a garter to get off my wife's leg!"

"Oh, for heaven's sake," Cami laughed. "Use the speaker, honey." She shook her head patiently at her new husband's antics.

Brant leaned back as the limo pulled away from the church. Out the window, Cami yelled happily that she'd see all the guests at the Double D. Dan pressed a wildly rambunctious kiss against Cami's cheek.

"Be careful of my veil, honey!" Cami admonished him, but he completely ignored her, pulling her into his lap for a smacking kiss that she seemed only too happy to participate in.

Brant turned to roll his eyes at Grace, but she was looking out the other window. It made him wonder if she was enjoying this wedding circus. He expected her to look wistful, maybe even envious.

Actually, though she obviously was happy for Cami, she seemed plainly immune to the event itself.

More to the point, she seemed completely immune to *him*.

THE GUESTS MILLED through the Durning house and over the grounds, apparently thrilled with the wedding buffet goodies the Yellowjacket Cafe had provided. Grace wasn't sure how Maggie had managed to do this much. She wandered over to her friend to compliment her.

"This is delicious, Maggie," she told her, gesturing with the plate she'd emptied. "You did a wonderful job." Her gaze swept the outdoor buffet tables, which were draped with tulle and flowers and lots of steaming food.

"Thanks, Grace. You just remember that when it's time to put out some calls for bids on your wedding." Maggie gave her a playful smile.

Grace's stomach pitched. "I think you're safe for a long time, Maggie. But I wouldn't dream of not throwing my business your way. After all, one day I'll probably be fitting *you* for a wedding gown, won't I?"

"Touché." Her friend looked pensive for a moment. "I'll tell you a secret, if you promise not to tell a soul. *Not a soul.*"

"I promise." She turned curious eyes on Maggie.

"I mean it, because this would really hurt John's feelings." At Grace's reassuring nod, Maggie said, "John asked me to marry him a long time ago. He's always wanted to get married."

Grace's jaw dropped. "What's all this macho posturing about never getting to the altar all about?"

Maggie shrugged. "Saving face, I guess. You tell a man no, and what're they supposed to do? Tell all his friends you turned him down?" She turned over some fruit on the buffet, making sure it was chilling evenly. "I don't mind his blustering, anyway. It suits me for folks to think he's the one who doesn't want to get hitched.'' She met Grace's eyes. "It ain't good to have a man's pride beat down.''

Grace hardly knew what to say. "Maggie Mason! I can't believe you've kept this a secret from me all this time.''

"I bet you'll be hearing that yourself from Brant before the night's over." Maggie's gaze slid meaningfully toward Brant, who was introducing his mother and her new husband to some guests.

Grace didn't want to think about that right now. Her stomach turned again, painfully. "How did you get all this done, Maggie? The ice sculptures are stunning, the decorations are perfect—"

"I leased out for the ice sculptures, and I hired extra help for the food and decorations. I intended to be mostly a guest tonight, and enjoy being with my friends. Don't change the subject." At Grace's guilty expression, she said, "I just want you to be prepared, Grace. I think Brant's going to be a bit hot that you kept the truth from him.''

"I had my reasons.'' She felt like crying. It was true, but she dreaded the moment.

"Don't let it go any longer than this weekend, Grace.'' Maggie rubbed her back soothingly. "I'm sure I'll hear the blowup clean over at my place.''

"I hope I'm not interrupting anything, ladies.'' Brant came to stand beside Grace, and she instantly stiffened with dread. "You two look so serious, I wanted to remind you that this is a joyous occasion. Maggie, the guests are raving about the food. I appreciate you doing this on short notice for us.''

"You're welcome, Brant.'' Maggie shot Grace a warning glance as she moved away, saying, "I was happy to do it. Anytime.''

Maggie's absence left Grace standing with a handsome Brant. She couldn't have imagined he would look so attractive in a formal tux, but the dark color set off the blackness of his hair and the deep blue of his eyes. Why had this man always been the only one who could set her heart to thundering?

"Let's take a walk, Grace." Brant took her arm gently, leading her away from the wedding party. "It's such a nice night, and I haven't spent two seconds alone with you."

Her guilty conscience sent prickles throughout her stomach, though she allowed him to lead her toward a paddock. "Cami lucked into wonderful weather for an outdoor wedding," she remarked, telling herself to keep her voice slow and steady.

He drew her to him as he leaned against a split rail fence. Tucking a strand of hair behind her ear that a mischievous May breeze was tugging at, Brant looked into her eyes. Grace's heart rate picked up enough that it was hard to breathe.

"Grace, I couldn't help thinking about us while we were standing at the altar tonight. I don't want to wait any longer to marry you." He hesitated, before saying, "The longer we wait, the more gossip it's going to cause. And I really believe that our place is with each other."

Putting a finger over her lips to stop her protest, Brant said, "You have every right to be sore at me for what I said in the hotel in New York. I didn't mean that I was going to have to marry you, but my mouth spoke before my brain had a chance to operate. And I know I'm not saying all this as pretty as it should be, but Grace, I want you."

Before she could react, he'd leaned his head forward, touching his lips to hers. Grace could do nothing but close her eyes and enjoy the kiss. It felt so good when he slid his arms around her, deepening the kiss. The sun was going down, sending gentle rays of heat upon them, and she could hear distant birds cawing at each other—and ringing in her ears. Sighing, she leaned into him, her hands automatically reaching to hold him closer to her.

Far-off laughter from the party guests floated their way. Brant gently broke off the kiss, his smile reluctant as he stared down at her. "Sounds like somebody else has decided to find a moment alone together."

She could barely nod as she ever so slightly separated herself from him.

"So, what's it going to be, Grace?"

Keeping her eyes trained on the starched shirt of his tux, Grace shook her head. "Brant, I'm sorry. I can't even think about anything like marriage right now."

Taking her chin between his fingers, Brant tipped her head to look into her eyes. "When do you think you will be able to? We don't have a whole lot of time, Grace."

They had less than he knew. Unhappily she stepped away from him, brushing at her skirt. "I've done a lot of thinking about it this week, Brant. I don't know why. Maybe it was seeing you and Cami so upset about your folks. It might have been...other things going through my mind. But I know that I can't marry you. Not now."

She shook her head at him before he could interrupt. "It's not a matter anymore of whether or not you would have ever asked me. It's knowing that it would hurt me too much when you decide you can't handle being tied down. Wait. Hear me out,'' she said in defense of the explosion she could feel he was about to have. ''You and Cami have been the most miserable people this week because your parents were coming, and they weren't arriving as a couple. It hurt *me* just to watch the two of you suffer so much, Brant!''

She cast pleading eyes on him, seeing the mutinous look growing there. ''Please, Brant. Think ahead. If you feel it's going to be hard on the baby if his parents don't get married, think about how much worse it's going to be if we don't *stay* married.'' Taking a deep breath, she said, ''In light of the fact that you just recently found out you are going to be a father, my gut feeling is that you're rushing to make things right, and that you might regret it later.'' She backed away from him slowly. ''Let's take a little more time to think about this, okay? A little more time to smooth over some of the rough spots.''

He advanced on her. ''How much time?''

Thinking guiltily of her due date, Grace turned her head and began heading toward the house. He caught up, grabbing her arm to slow her down. ''How much time?''

''I'm...not sure. We'll know when the time is right,'' she stammered.

He pulled her to a complete stop. ''I'm going to have to think about this, Grace Barclay. I have the strangest feeling you're putting me off. For the life of me, I can't figure out why.''

''I told you,'' she insisted.

His eyes narrowed and he released her. ''Don't

forget I'm driving you home tonight, Grace. Don't you dare find a way to disappear on me. You and I are not through talking.''

He tapped her lips lightly with a finger, before slipping an arm through hers to escort her back to the party. Grace pasted a happy smile on her face, but the truth was, she felt ill. Near the buffet tables, Maggie sent her a questioning look. Grace shook her head, receiving a you-gotta-tell-him eyebrow raise from her friend.

She'd had all she could stand. Depositing Brant near guests she knew he would have to speak to, she headed into the house. Running up the stairs to the room where she had dressed for the wedding that afternoon, she closed the door and threw herself on the bed.

Cheerful voices floated in through the window, but Grace closed her eyes. She'd had all the wedding euphoria she could stand for tonight. She was delighted for Cami's sake, but Grace knew her moment of reckoning would arrive with the tossing of the birdseed on the departing bride and groom.

GRACE MUST HAVE SLEPT, because all of sudden Cami was shaking her awake.

"Grace! Are you all right?" Cami's distressed face was so at odds with the beauty of the wedding veil above it that Grace felt terrible for upsetting her friend.

"I'm fine." She pushed herself to a sitting position. "I just got tired and came up here for a nap."

"It's a good thing you did, but you missed out on the cake! Oh, well, there's lots left!" Cami gave her a playful pat on the arm. "Are you up to getting me out of this dress? It's time."

"Time!" She lumbered off the bed. "Goodness! Turn around so I can unbutton your dress."

While Grace worked on the back, Elsa Durning entered the room, going without a word to unpin the veil from Cami's hair. "I don't think I've ever seen a prettier veil, Cami," she murmured. "You are a lovely bride."

"Thanks, Mom." In the mirror, Grace could see Cami's eyes glowing with happiness. "Grace insisted on this veil."

Elsa met Grace's eyes without hesitation. Unspoken thoughts lay in Elsa's eyes, which Grace could read very well. Now was not the time, but she realized Elsa was not leaving Fairhaven without having a talk with her. Grace sighed, knowing she would do no less if she were in Elsa's shoes.

"It's lovely, Grace," Elsa commented without any inflection. "Thank you for helping my daughter."

Between them, they wiggled Cami out of her dress and undergarments. "That reminds me!" she exclaimed. "I have something for you, Grace."

Cami hurried over to her dresser and took a small, silver-wrapped box out of a drawer. "Here," she said, handing the tiny package to Grace. "For the world's greatest maid of honor."

Tears sprang into Grace's eyes. "I didn't do that much, Cami."

"Well, open it!"

Grace met Elsa's eyes over the box. Though Grace felt that they should be dressing Cami for her no doubt impatient groom, Elsa seemed to be waiting to see what the box contained. Hurriedly she unwrapped the box and gasped.

"Oh, Cami! You shouldn't have." Grace adored the gold circle pin, surrounded with tiny pearls. "I love it!" She leaned to give Cami a hug, careful of both their stomachs. The women laughed, and Cami took the pin from her to attach it to Grace's dress.

"There." She shrugged at Grace. "I hope it brings you good luck and the same happiness I've found."

It was plain that Cami was wishing Grace good luck with working everything out with Brant. Considering her condition, Grace blushed a little under Elsa's watchful eyes. "Thank you, Cami."

Quickly Elsa and Grace finished dressing Cami. Without further delay, the bride hugged them both, then ran down the stairs to meet her groom. Laughing, the other two women followed. Cami ran to kiss her father, and then Brant. Someone pressed a tulle birdseed bag into Grace's hand, and she joined in throwing it on the departing couple. For the first time, sentimental tears jumped into Grace's eyes as the limo pulled away, with Cami and Dan waving goodbye.

"That's that, I guess," she murmured to herself.

A gentle, but determined hand closed around her upper arm. "Not quite," said Elsa Durning.

Chapter Fifteen

"If you have a moment, Grace, I would like to speak with you."

Grace sighed inwardly, recognizing Durning determination in Elsa's eyes. "All right."

Elsa took her into a parlor room off the hall, motioning her to take a seat. Reluctantly Grace complied.

"Grace, I guess I feel that before I go, I should welcome you into the family. Whether or not you and Brant ever marry is a personal decision the two of you will have to deal with, but married or not, you are still carrying my grandchild."

She paused, giving Grace a chance to register her words. "If there is anything I can do to help you, I hope that you'll feel free to ask me."

"There isn't, but I appreciate your offer." She couldn't meet the older woman's eyes with comfort.

"I see. Well, I suppose I'm not far off the mark to suggest that I'll be returning to Fairhaven in a few weeks."

She directed a pointed stare at Grace's stomach, telling her silently that she might have fooled Brant, but his mother wasn't as gullible. Grace didn't offer a denial of Elsa's statement. "Will you have help of any kind with the baby?"

"My sister, Hope, is coming to stay with me."

"For a few days?"

"For the summer. I'll need help running the shop for a while, and also taking care of the baby."

"Hmm." Elsa's eyebrows raised. "If you have Hope living with you, obviously you and Brant are not planning on a household arrangement other than the one you have right now."

She was asking, basically, if the two of them were planning to live together. Grace couldn't blame Brant's mother for being curious, especially as the two of them weren't planning the same sentimental wedding Cami and Dan had chosen.

"No. I'm sure Brant has his hands full with the ranch, and I like where I live."

"Well." Mrs. Durning stood. "Certainly things have changed since I was a girl. I don't know what to make of everything, to be honest." Her gray-blue eyes, a more faded version of Brant's, looked at Grace without a hint of disapproval. "Expecting two grandbabies in the same year has me flustered, not to mention the unusual circumstances. But," she said with a shake of her head, "maybe it's better for you young people to be sure you know your mind. Divorce is difficult. If you honestly feel that you and Brant are not meant to be together, then perhaps you are being wise and mature." She pursed her lips before looking steadfastly at Grace. "However, the fact that you will not join the Durning family in name doesn't mean that I will think less of, nor spend less time with, this particular grandchild. I hope you will understand when I return in, what, two weeks?"

Her guess was a calculated question. "Yes," Grace replied, knowing she had to be truthful with Elsa.

"I will want to see my grandchild. I will probably be underfoot. If the mountain will not come to Mohammed, I will be at your house every day with a burp cloth in my hand. It will not be to press you about Brant, because I intend to stay out of your business. But please," she said softly, her eyes earnest, "let me know my grandchild."

Tears sprang into Grace's eyes. "You're welcome at my house anytime."

"Thank you," Elsa whispered. Without warning, she drew Grace into a hug, startling her. "I've known your family for a long time, Grace. I'd love to treat you like a daughter now."

"I'd like that." More than anything, Grace appreciated Elsa's kindness. She had been so afraid of the unknown; now she could relax knowing that no matter what, she and her baby wouldn't be outcasts for not making a desperate dash to the altar.

"Elsa!" Dr. Nelson entered the room, knocking on the wood paneling to announce his arrival. "I've been looking all over for you. I was afraid you'd holed up somewhere, crying sentimental tears over Cami leaving."

"No." Elsa sniffled, but offered him a smile. "What's to cry about that?"

"I don't know." He looked from Grace to Elsa. "I thought perhaps because your only daughter just left the nest."

"Oh, but she didn't," Elsa said with a meaningful look at Grace. "Come on, Bob. It's time to say goodnight to the guests."

AN HOUR LATER, Grace stood waiting in the hallway for Brant to take her home. She had helped Maggie put trays and food away, despite her protests. Finally Brant told her in no uncertain terms to go get her things. Grace had been glad to acquiesce, realizing that the euphoria of a lovely wedding was wearing off and she simply needed to get home.

"I think that's everyone," Brant said, coming to join her in the hallway. Bob and Elsa had made their way upstairs, the last guest was gone and it was just the two of them standing under the foyer chandelier. "Mission accomplished."

"Yes." She offered him a tentative smile.

"You know," he said, cocking his head to listen, "this house already sounds different."

"What do you mean?"

"It's...silent."

"It is after midnight," Grace said softly.

"No, it's not that. I think—" Brant hesitated, looking over his shoulder. "I'm used to listening for Cami. She's usually got the TV running, or a radio going full-blast on a country and western station, or something mixing in the kitchen. But it's...quiet now."

"You're going to miss her, aren't you?" Grace felt a sympathetic twinge for this big macho man who had just watched his sister leave.

"Well, it won't be the Double D Ranch any-more," he said, trying to sound matter-of-fact. She heard the strain in his voice, and knew he was trying to underplay his feelings. "It'll be just a single D. One Durning. No plural, unless, of course, you've changed your mind?"

"I don't think so, Brant." Her eyes lowered to the marble floor beneath her feet.

"Come on, then," he said gruffly. "I'll take you home."

They were silent on the return drive. She couldn't help thinking that life had changed very fast for Brant; he was going to have a lot to get used to very soon. Without his sister around to poke at him, he was going to have way too much time to brood. He was probably too keyed up after the wedding to be able to sleep tonight. She certainly was.

As he pulled in the driveway in back of her house, Grace took a deep breath and a plunge she hadn't planned on. "Would you like to come in for a night-cap?"

Surprise lifted his brows. "Really?"

"Yes, really." Grace smiled at him. "I can't bear to think of you all alone at your house tonight."

"I won't be alone," he grumbled. "It's hard as hell to think about Bob and Mom sleeping upstairs together."

She had forgotten all about that. "Well, come on in. I'll get you a fortifying beer."

Sliding out of the truck, she heard him following behind her. They went inside her house, and Grace flipped on a few lights as she walked through to the kitchen. "Oh, I'm glad to be home," she murmured. Grabbing him a beer out of the fridge that had been left from the previous weekend's barbecue, she said, "Make yourself comfortable. I'm going to change out of this dress, if you don't mind."

"Take your time." Brant accepted the beer and walked into the den where they'd unwrapped the bassinet last weekend. "I was sure glad to get out of my monkey suit."

"Brant." Grace laughed. "How could you call that exquisite tuxedo such a thing? Cami worked hard choosing an outfit that would complement your masculine image."

"What's that supposed to mean?"

She laughed again as she headed up the stairs. "Originally she picked out baby blue for her wedding colors. You would have worn a silver suit—"

"Over my dead body," Brant yelled up after her.

"She said that would be your reaction." Grace grinned as she unzipped her dress. Slipping into an oversize shirt and baggy shorts, she breathed a deep sigh of relief. It wasn't true, of course, about the silver tux, but she and Cami had enjoyed a good laugh over austere Brant wearing one. Brushing the hair spray from her hair, Grace let it fall soft and loose around her face, not even wanting a rubber band pulling at her after being in panty hose all day.

"Maternity panty hose is a cruel and unusual punishment," she muttered as she went downstairs. Getting a cold glass of water from the tap, she joined Brant in the living room. "Sausage casings would be more comfortable."

She hadn't sat close to him, so he scooted closer to her. Grace leaned into him, suddenly too tired and too needful of his strength to pull away. "Your mother and I had a nice talk tonight."

"Hmm. I should have warned you. I got mine last night. Grace," he said, tipping her head back so he could look into her eyes, "this is our decision. Mom means well, but I'm willing to go at your pace for a while longer, if need be."

"Really?"

"Yes. Really." He leaned to drop a soft kiss against her lips. "I'm not happy about it," he murmured. "I'm old-fashioned enough to believe that being a father means I ought to be a husband, too. But I'm not going anywhere, Grace. Not this time."

She moaned under his lips as he kissed her again. He traveled from her lips over to her cheeks, and down her neck. One hand pressed at her back to support her, the other pushed her hair gently from her face. The kiss left her breathless, and wanting. She had wanted this man for so long. "Stay the night," she whispered.

Hesitating, Brant checked her expression. "I can sleep on the sofa, if you just don't want to be alone tonight."

"You'll like my bed better."

"I know, but—" Brant took her hand and pressed it to his lips. "Are you sure?"

"I'm sure." Grace rose, pulling him with her. "This feels very right to me."

He allowed her to pull him up the stairs into the bedroom, where only the small nightstand lamp sent comforting light into the darkness. She leaned against him, this time wrapping her arms around his neck to join them together for a long kiss.

"Oh, Grace," he murmured against her mouth. "Won't I hurt you? Or the baby?"

"Not if we're careful."

He glanced at the double bed doubtfully. "I'm not sure this is a good idea. There isn't room for three in that bed. We might squash him."

She laughed softly, her fingers nimbly unbuttoning the casual Western shirt he wore. Guiding his hands to her T-shirt, Grace silently showed him that everything was going to be fine. Very carefully, he removed her top, running his hands along the smoothness of her back.

"Grace, you feel so good," he said on a husky whisper. "As crazy as it sounds, I remember your skin being this silky. You feel just the same."

"Just bigger," she murmured.

He chuckled, undoing her bra and sliding that off, too. Taking his time, he kissed his way down to her breasts. "Maybe."

"Maybe!" Grace laughed, giving him a gentle push onto the bed. "Brant Durning, I'm a lot bigger up top."

"It's kind of…interesting," he said, catching her to him.

She felt her skin heating wherever he kissed her. Without worry that he wouldn't find her attractive, Grace slid out of her shorts, and helped him take off the rest of his clothes.

"So that's the baby," he said, his eyes wide as he ran one hand over her stomach. "Made himself right at home, little dickens. I don't believe there's another spare inch in there."

Reality swiftly intruded. She opened her mouth to tell him the truth, but he was putting sweet kisses on her stomach before kissing her lips again. Sighing with happiness, she gave herself up into the wonder of being in Brant's arms again.

Pleasure cascaded over her as they joined together. "I've missed you so much," she whispered.

"I was wrong, Grace." He moved inside her, burying his face in her hair. "I shouldn't have acted the way I did."

"Shh. Let's not think about that right now." She couldn't. She didn't want to. Spasms built inside her, and she clung to Brant's strong-muscled back in wonder.

"Oh, Brant..."

Her moan was against his mouth as he took her lips with fast, passionate kisses. "Oh, Brant!"

It just about killed him, but he stopped. "Am I hurting you?"

She shook her head wildly. "Don't stop," she begged.

He allowed himself to relax at her words. Stunned by the force building inside him, he felt Grace's climax, and that was all it took to send him over the edge into her arms.

They lay together, enjoying the feeling of being entwined.

"I've missed you," he told her, rolling gently to one side so he wouldn't crush her or the baby. "I never forgot how wonderful you feel when we make love."

Unease tugged at Grace. It had been more than wonderful; there had been an emotional power in their lovemaking that had been stronger than anything she'd ever felt. Maybe it was the baby making her sentimental. Maybe it was the joy of being with Brant again. But for now, she couldn't bear to spoil the beauty of the moment.

In the morning, she would tell him the truth.

IN THE MORNING, Grace rose and got dressed, admiring Brant as he slept in her canopied bed. She went downstairs and fixed some breakfast, still glowing from last night. If only...if only there wasn't one major problem in their way.

"Good morning," a voice said, just as warm arms encircled her. She squealed, jumping.

"Brant! I didn't hear you come down."

He grinned, more handsome than ever with his black hair tousled from sleep and his blue eyes lit with playful laughter. "You were obviously somewhere else."

Handing him a glass of orange juice and a plate of toast, she ushered him into the living room.

"Hey, I peeked into the nursery. Looks great. Maggie and Tilly can do just about anything, can't they?"

"Yes." They could, but nobody could help her with what needed to be done now. "Brant, we have to talk."

"Talk?" His expression was instantly wary. "It's not the baby—"

"It isn't anything to do with the baby. Well, it is, a little," she added hastily.

"Why don't you just say what's on your mind?" he asked quietly. "Obviously this is delicate subject matter. I'm listening."

"Brant, I didn't tell you the truth about my due date." Uncomfortably she watched his expression change to disbelief as his gaze ricocheted from her face to her stomach.

"Was my mother right?"

She nodded. "If she told you I'm due sooner than later, she was right."

He put the glass of orange juice back on the table. "How soon?"

"Maybe two weeks."

"Two weeks! Grace Barclay, what about last night?"

"Last night was wonderful."

"I know that, but we could have put the baby at risk!"

"Dr. Delancey said making love was fine as long as I felt good."

"I just got back last month! Why would he have been discussing sex with you?"

"It's probably something all doctors mention to their pregnant patients, along with the rest of the laundry list they have."

Jumping to his feet, he paced the room. "Why didn't you tell me the truth?"

Grace rubbed her hands over her wrists nervously. "I didn't want you to feel pressured. Not any more than you did."

"Pressured! Who feels pressured?" He paced a few more times. "I do. I feel pressured! You said we had a couple of months."

"I know. I'm sorry."

"And I said—" Brant ignored her "—I said I was willing to go at your pace."

"That's right. I didn't want to have to speed anything up."

"I don't think we have to worry about that, Grace. If you're going to have that baby any day now, the time for pacing ourselves is past."

"No, it's not. That's exactly what I wanted to avoid. Brant, my feelings haven't changed."

His jaw jutted, his expression turning stubborn. "I can't believe I'm hearing this."

"Look." A defensive streak hit her out of nowhere. "I waited for you to ask me to marry you. I knew I was pregnant. By the third month, when I knew I couldn't wait much longer before I started showing, I mentioned marriage. I got a good look at your backside rushing from my bedroom for my trouble. Six months later you resurface, discover you're going to be a father, and expect me to gladly march down the aisle."

"Grace! It wasn't the way it's done. The man is supposed to ask the woman!"

"Oh, pardon me if I intruded on some medieval tenet of the Chauvinist Bylaws," she spat. "I didn't realize I was intruding on your sense of correctness by inquiring as to whether your intentions were honorable, Brant Durning. Of course, if we're going to reach that far back into etiquette past, you should have asked me to marry you *before* you made love to me."

"My intentions were always honorable!"

"Oh, I see. You intended to marry me all the time. You just didn't want to talk about it."

"I—I," he sputtered. "I hadn't thought about it, Grace. But my intentions were honorable!"

She hurt, just as much as she had when he'd walked out several months ago. He wasn't about to see her point at all, which was why she couldn't just fall in with what he wanted now. "You have something very basic confused here, Brant, but it doesn't matter. I'm sorry if it's inconvenient that our baby is coming a few weeks earlier than you'd gotten used to—"

"A few weeks!"

She ignored the interruption. "But you have just proved my case all over again. Instantly you want to leap into the courthouse to buy a marriage license, because you've discovered Junior's on the way. Well, I'm not going.'' With a taut sob, she instinctively covered her stomach with her hand, as if to apologize to the life inside her for having to hear its parents argue so bitterly. ''What you're asking me is to take you back, Brant. The problem is, we can't go backward.''

''I don't like any of this, Grace.'' He grabbed his keys, which he'd thrown on the coffee table last night. ''I'm going to have to think about this. Obviously I wasn't prepared to be lied to. You'd already deceived me, Lord only knows when you'd intended to tell me about my child. I'm sorry, but all I know is, I gotta have some fresh air.''

He jogged upstairs to get the rest of his clothes, hurrying back down to stalk to the door. ''I'll pick you up for dinner tonight, when your shop closes. You and I have a lot to talk about, I think it's safe to say.''

''Fine!'' Hurt, anxious, self-righteous tears stung her eyes.

''Fine.'' He shot her a hard look, one that contained disbelief and betrayal, and closed the door behind him.

It was too much for Grace. She hurried up the stairs and flung herself onto the bed. The sound of his truck engine being gunned flooded through her window, before she heard it pull down the driveway.

Brant was furious. She had known he would be. Between now and dinnertime, she needed to think of a way to salvage this mess.

She still couldn't say yes, though right now, she doubted very much if Brant would be interested in restating his offer.

"THAT COTTON-PICKIN' WOMAN," Brant grumbled to a sympathetic Maggie and John. "She's got me tied in so many knots, I feel like a lariat."

"Love's a many-splendored thing," Maggie said sympatheticall', "but only if it's working out for ya."

"It hasn't ever worked out for me where Grace is concerned."

That bothered him. It really did. He wasn't the kind, sensitive type of individual she seemed to want. Self-pity filled him. "Heckfire! Grace knew what I was about when she got involved with me. I asked her out, you know, but she didn't have to say yes."

"Probably shouldn't have," Maggie told him.

"I'll tell you something." He looked up to meet the warm acceptance in his friends' eyes. "I'm glad about the baby. I'm real glad about it. I may not be beans as a date, but I'll be a great father. I've decided to." He might make some mistakes along the parenting line, but he wasn't going to struggle with it the way his father had. When the boy needed a pat on the back, Brant was going to give it to him. Then an extra one, just in case there was any misunderstanding of how proud he was of his child.

"Don't say that, Brant." Maggie squeezed his arm. "You're a good man. You and Grace just went at this a little crossways. It'll all work out, I'm sure it will."

"Yeah. Well, I'm not so sure." He got heavily to his feet. "I'm off. I just wanted to stop in and thank you for all your help with Cami's wedding before I got on home to my chores."

John and Maggie nodded as he walked to the door. "See ya, Purvis, Buzz."

The men mumbled a goodbye at him without their customary enthusiasm. They barely glanced up from their checkerboard. Brant's heart sank. Nobody seemed to know what to say to him. Even he didn't know what to say about the problem he had on his hands.

SOMETIME BETWEEN the time Brant was picking up litter that had floated down from the party into the pastures, and the time he was making his bed, he discerned one important thing. Grace wanted him in her life, that was clear from last night. They were going to be together forever, whether they were married or not, though he didn't think that should be the case. But with the baby coming, she would need help.

She was going to need *him*. That necessitated a gift, a practical gift, that a woman like Grace clearly would understand was a peace offering. She would clearly know that, for now, he was still trying to be utmost patient with her.

That was one thing he knew he had to be. Brant had gone to the bookstore this morning after he'd stopped at the Yellowjacket, and bought out half the titles on expecting a baby. Each and every one of the first chapters of those books preached the rewards a man could reap if he was patient and sensitive to his partner's needs. Apparently a pregnant woman had so many different changes going on inside her body that the rest of her life needed to stay on as even a keel as possible.

That sounded reasonable to Brant. Though patience wasn't his strong suit—especially now that the window of opportunity had closed up on him significantly, he could be supportive. He could be helpful.

To Brant, the way was clear. Grace needed a bigger bed.

Chapter Sixteen

Brant made sure he picked Grace up on time at the Wedding Wonderland. She didn't seem pleased to see him as he poked his head in the shop, but he told himself that within the next half hour, everything would be smoothed over between them.

"Ready?" he asked her.

"Let me lock up." Her back was stiff, her eyes unwelcoming.

"Are you hungry?"

She didn't turn to look at him. "A little, but I'd like to change before we go eat. If that's all right with you."

"I'm in no rush." Actually, it might even work in with his plans.

They drove in silence to Grace's house. She hopped out and went to the back door. "That's strange," she murmured. "I know I locked this door when I left."

He shrugged, his expression innocent. "I read that pregnant women can start getting forgetful, they've got so much on their minds thinking about the baby and all."

She gave him a narrow glance but said nothing as she went inside.

"Do you want me to check around and make sure there's no burglars?"

"No, thanks. I must have just forgotten to lock the door," she called, heading up the stairs. "I'll just be a second."

Exactly one second later a blood-curdling shriek resounded from upstairs. Brant shot up the staircase and hurried to Grace.

She was staring at a California king-size bed. It took up nearly every inch of her bedroom, which meant there'd be plenty of room for him, Grace and Brant Junior.

He glanced at Grace. Her mouth twitched spasmodically, but no sound was coming out. Of course, the bed was completely bare of sheets. Brant hadn't had time to make it. By the horrified look on Grace's face, he wondered belatedly if he should have taken the time to do so. "Do you like it?"

Grace leaned against the wall, her eyes riveted to the bed. "What in the world is that awful thing? Did you do this, Brant Wyndford Durning?"

"Yes." His heart sank at her adjective. "You don't like it."

"Where is my bed?" Those hazel eyes of hers looked like chips of uncrackable ice.

"In the nursery," he said practically. "The baby can sleep in it when he's bigger."

"This is the ugliest thing I ever saw!" she said between gritted teeth. "What could possibly have possessed you to think I would want such a monstrosity?"

"Grace, you're going to need help with the baby."

His tone was reasoning, placating, as he might speak to a mare gone wild. "Now, I understand that you're not ready to come to terms with getting to the altar, and in your condition, I can see why you'd want to wait. But I need to be here to help you."

"My sister will be here," Grace hissed.

Brant didn't see that as a problem at all. "She'll need someplace to sleep, then. Might as well be close to the baby."

"I don't think you're hearing me, Brant Durning," Grace said, her hands on her hips. "You can't just move in here. Making love last night was not an invitation to move your boots under my bed permanently."

"Wait a minute, Grace." Brant tried to control the anger that wanted to surface, but the woman was confusing him. "We're having a baby. That means our lives are connected for the rest of our days. Now, I'm trying to understand your reasons for not wanting to marry me. I'm really trying to be patient." He drew in a deep, calming breath. "I *really* am. But you cannot expect me to jump in the sack with you every time the urge hits you, then kick me out every morning. We need more of a relationship than that. *I* need more."

"How dare you?" Grace advanced on him to jab a finger against his shoulder in feminine rage. "You sneak into my house without my permission to have the most atrocious bed I've ever seen delivered so we can have a relationship? This bed," she shrieked, gathering steam, "no doubt, was trundled past the Yellowjacket and parked outside my house for everyone in Fairhaven *to see what the father of my child thinks enough of me to consider a gift?*"

The last words sounded like a near-scream. Brant reminded himself that the books called for patience. Trying again, he said, "I thought you didn't care about gossip." She had reprimanded him for caring too much about what people thought several times. "Besides, when the baby is born, I'm afraid I'll roll over on him."

"I hadn't planned on three of us sleeping in a bed!" Grace retorted.

His mouth fell open as the implication of her words sank in. "You don't want me to help you at night with the baby?" He couldn't comprehend that. All the baby books said the first month could be rough with extra feedings and diaper changing, and maybe even colic. Brant knew all about colic from having horses. You had to walk those suckers, and keep walking 'em, even when you were dead-tired and the horse wanted to quit. He'd figured on doing the same with his boy.

"I will have Hope to help me." Grace bit off the words. Her expression was taut and drawn, implacable.

Full realization of what she was saying dawned unpleasantly for Brant. "You haven't planned much on me being around, have you? You've got everything taken care of."

Hurt feelings forced him to hope that Grace would smile now and say there was something in his baby's life she was counting on him helping with. When she said nothing, keeping her furious gaze locked with his, indignation blew up his pride. "All right. If that's the way you want it, Grace. Obviously this is my punishment for being unable to meet your previous timetable for a wedding." He shot her a disbelieving look over his shoulder as he headed down the stairs. "I'll call the furniture store and have the bed taken back. But I won't be calling you again. If you're determined to have this baby without me, there's not much I can do except stay out of your way."

He hurried to his truck, unable to ignore the burning in his eyes. The only place he knew to go where he could sit and be among people who at least had a kind word for him was the Yellowjacket. Parking his truck out front, he went inside, throwing himself into a booth in the back.

Maggie came over at once, closing the red wooden blinds against the last rays of afternoon summer sun. "Howdy, Brant. How's life treating you?"

"So good I'll take a glass of your tea to celebrate."

By the uh-uh rise in her eyebrows, Brant figured Maggie had heard the sarcasm in his voice. Giving him a la-di-da shake of her head, she went off to get his tea.

Sheriff John Farley cruised in the door a second later, while Brant was morosely examining the cracks in the old wooden table. He spied Brant in the back of the Cafe.

"Hey!" he shouted, taking off his hat. "Hell of an engagement ring you had delivered to Grace, Brant."

Brant let his head sink onto his palm. He refused to reply, especially with Buzz and Purvis and everyone else in the restaurant looking up at John's ribbing.

"I came here to be amongst friends," he replied sternly, "not amateur comedians."

"Naw." John slid into the booth across from him. "You came here because Grace gave you a good, swift kick in the pants. Man, are you confused." He laughed heartily at Brant's scowl. "Did it ever occur to you to buy the woman an engagement ring instead of a place to park your butt?"

"I bought one of those, too," Brant said, morosely flipping out a ring box. "The woman hasn't been in the mood to accept it, yet. Keeps telling me that she won't marry me." He set the velvet ring box on the table between them and sighed deeply, running a hand through his hair in agitation. "The baby books say I need to be patient. I'm trying, I really am. It's just so hard."

Maggie walked over with the tea, instantly snatching the box up the second her eyes lit on it. Flipping it open, she gasped at what lay inside. John craned to look at it, too.

"Damn, Brant," he said, "there's a difference between patience and idiocy. That diamond would have got you a yes out of Grace for sure."

He shook his head. "You don't know Grace. Once she makes up her mind, it's made up. There aren't any if, ands or buts. And if the woman says she's not saying yes, I could give her Queen Elizabeth's tiara and she'd slap it on my head, instead."

"I don't know." Maggie closed the box with a snap and put it back on the table. "Sure is a pretty ring, Brant. Gotta say you picked out a beauty, though I can't say I would have expected you to ante up for such a big one."

"Didn't want her to have less than Cami got." He scowled at the table, not seeing the cracks anymore. "Three months ago, I probably wouldn't have bought it. But I thought Dan probably knew a little bit better at romancing a woman than I did. After all, he managed to end up at the altar while I'm still wearing egg on my face.''

Maggie slid into the seat next to him. ''There's no egg on your face,'' she said softly. ''All of us around here, we think you're doing the right thing. We think you've tried awful hard to make inroads, Brant, even if your methods are a bit screwy at times.''

''Tell that to Grace. Where she's concerned, I can't do anything right.''

''No, now I can't tell Grace anything, hon. We happen to think she's done her best to cope with what she had, what she thought she was gonna have. All I'm saying,'' Maggie said, reaching to put a comforting hand over Brant's, ''is that neither of you is wearing egg. It's gotten a little rocky for the two of you, but ain't nothing worth having if you don't have to work for it.''

Brant snorted. ''Having Grace say yes without bucking me anymore would be just fine.''

Maggie patted his hand silently. John opened the box again, shaking his head as he stared at the ring. Nobody said anything, and Brant figured everything that could be said, had been.

Except yes.

MUCH TO GRACE'S DISMAY, Brant was at the Yellowjacket. She'd seen his truck parked outside. After a moment's indecision, she hurried in the door. She needed to talk to Maggie, urgently.

The Cafe owner greeted her, taking her to a booth at the front to sit. ''Darn big crib Brant had delivered to your house today,'' she said softly.

"It's not funny, Maggie." Grace could feel Brant staring at her. She wasn't about to turn around. "Don't you even mention that horrible thing to me."

"Aw, honey, maybe it isn't so bad."

"You haven't seen it!" Grace shook her head. "I didn't come to talk about that. I have a question."

"Coulda called me over the phone, Grace." Maggie cast worried eyes on her.

"I...knew you'd be getting busy with supper rush." Besides, Grace had desperately wanted to discuss the situation privately, where she knew kitchen help wouldn't be running around bothering Maggie.

"Maggie," she whispered, "I've got a stomachache."

Her friend pinned laser-intense eyes on her. "What kind of stomachache?"

"Just a strange...unusual stomach. I didn't think anything of it...particularly as I'd just seen Brant's delivery." Grace drew a deep breath. "I think I'm having contractions."

Maggie nodded at her struggle for definition. "That's normal. Have your waters broke?"

"No."

"All right." Maggie leaned back in the booth, her gaze flicking to the back of the Cafe. "This could be the beginning, but it still could be a day or two before anything significant starts happening."

"You don't think...I mean, Brant and I...we—"

"No." Maggie waved a hand at her dismissively. "Doubtful. Did anything hurt at the time?"

Grace shook her head. To the contrary, it had been exquisite.

"If you're real worried, you should put in a call

to Dr. Delancey. It's probably a good idea, anyway, as he might want to examine you."

"Okay." Grace wasn't all that worried, now that she'd had a dose of Maggie's common sense. Excitement and anticipation had flooded her to the point that she had to talk to her friend. Now, with more rational reasoning to work with, Grace could slow down enough to think straight.

"Phone's in the kitchen," Maggie said unnecessarily.

"Thanks." Grace got up and headed to the kitchen. She caught the doctor's office just before they closed. After a moment, Dr. Delancey came on the line.

"Think you're having some signals, Grace?" he asked kindly.

"I'm not sure." Her heart was fluttering. "I've had some off and on contractions for a few days, but this started out as a stomachache, and feels like it's progressing."

"Well, calm down," he told her, much in the same tone of voice Maggie had used with her. "You're probably just at the start of things. You could come in and let me check you, but frankly, with a first child, you could still have some time. You probably want to get poked at as little as possible."

"Yes." Grace could agree to that with ease.

"It's a nice evening. Why don't you go take a nice slow walk around the square, or do something else that might take your mind off of it? Sitting and worrying's not the best thing to do right now."

"That's a good idea." Grace couldn't imagine sitting. Suddenly she realized one thousand items that had to be crossed off her to-do list before this baby could be born. "Thank you, Dr. Delancey."

"You're welcome. I'll have my pager if you have any further questions. No matter the hour, Grace, if you get concerned about anything, you just call."

"Thank you," she repeated, hanging up.

Maggie came to stand at her side. "So?"

"I'm supposed to go take my mind off of it. How in the world can I do that? I've got a million things to do!"

Maggie laughed. "First thing you better do is tell the father not to leave town."

"Oh, my gosh!" Grace had forgotten about Brant glowering in the back of the Cafe. "I guess I'd better." She glanced his way, only to snag on his gaze. "Maybe not right now," she murmured. "I'll call him later. Bye, Maggie." Hurrying to the door, she called, "Thank you!"

"You want me to come by later?"

"What for?"

"Just to check on you?" Maggie's grin was broad.

"I'm fine," Grace called. "I'll call you when I start feeling like it's getting close. Dr. Delancey said this baby might take his sweet time about getting here."

She waved and hurried out the door. Not that she didn't appreciate Maggie's offer, but there was a lot Grace wanted to think about if Brant Junior was fixing to change her world around.

First, she had to alert Hope that she might be needed sooner than later. Brant's red truck caught her eye, slowing her feet. Brant had offered to be there for her. Did it really matter whether he was in her life just because of the baby?

Wasn't it more important that he wanted to be there?

"I DON'T KNOW what to do about those two," Maggie confessed to John. "They've got themselves tied up so well they can't find a way out of the knot."

"Not our place to do anything probably." John rubbed Maggie's shoulders as she walked him out to his cruiser. "Maybe we've meddled as much as we should."

"I suppose you're right. The horses have been led to water. Goodness knows, nobody can make them drink."

"You going up to Grace's later?"

Maggie squinted that direction. "I have a feeling she won't need my coaching until the morning. She said she would call me later. I expect she just wants some time to herself."

John got into the cruiser, rolling down the window. "Did she tell Brant?"

"Nope."

He scratched the back of his neck. "Well, I'll never figure women as long as I live."

She gave him a gentle slap on the arm. "Quit trying. We don't want to be figured."

Sighing, he said, "I don't guess anybody thinks the father would be interested in knowing he better wash up tonight and get some clothes ready and all, if his baby's fixing to come looking for him?"

"Grace didn't seem disposed to say anything to him."

"One part of me says we've meddled enough, Maggie Mason. The other part says those two are so stubborn, the only thing that would keep them together long enough to talk this out would be a locked jail cell.''

She gasped. ''You wouldn't!''

''I could.'' He sighed heavily. ''But I won't. Call me if you need anything.'' He pooched his lips out for his kiss goodbye. Maggie dropped a swift one on his mouth and hurried back inside, the idea of a jail cell intriguing her once she got past her initial shock.

''Maggie!'' an insistent male voice called from the back. Brant waved at her, so with a glance at the kitchen to make sure everything was proceeding as it should be, she headed to his table.

''What was that all about?'' he demanded. ''And don't tell me nothing, because I've got eyes in my head.''

''Really?'' she retorted. ''Then how come you're so blind?''

''What's that supposed to mean?'' He narrowed his gaze on her. The woman was keeping something from him, that was certain. Grace had likely put her up to it.

''I can't say. I shouldn't have said that. I think I've got nerves,'' Maggie replied, sounding shocked at the thought. ''I can't remember the last time I was nervous.''

''Is my baby on the way?''

She glanced at him in surprise. ''Why would you think that?''

''Grace came running in here like a wind had pushed her through the door, takes a few seconds to talk to you, then heads to the phone. Shortly thereafter, she's out of here like a shot.'' He wanted her to know he was paying attention. ''Not a word does she say to me, the father of the child and the last person she wants to be bothered with at this moment.''

"Brant, can I see you for a sec?'' Grace asked, appearing from behind Maggie's broad back.

Maggie and Brant both jumped guiltily. He had never even heard the Cafe door open.

"Uh, if Miss Maggie's through bending my ear,'' he said, trying to save face.

Maggie backed up. "I think our discussion's finished.'' She headed back to the kitchen, saying, "I'll get you a glass of water, Grace. It's getting mighty warm in here.''

"I'm sorry, Brant,'' Grace said without acknowledging Maggie's comment, nor sitting down. "I overreacted a little when I saw the bed. You're right. I can't expect you to sleep on the sofa after the baby comes. Nor should you and I be making love if I don't intend to marry you. I shouldn't have done it.''

Brant's heart had soared when he realized he was the willing recipient of an apology. But it had shattered at the rest of Grace's words. Now, he could only stare at her as he tried to understand what she was truly telling him.

"That's all I have to say.'' Whirling around, Grace started to hurry back on her way.

Brant grabbed her wrist before she could take two steps. "Oh, no, you don't, Grace Barclay. I didn't like the sound of that. Your behavior is making me very suspicious. You have two choices. Either you tell me what's going on right here, right now, or I take you home and you tell me there. It's your choice, but either way, I'm stuck to you like glue until I know.''

Chapter Seventeen

Grace leveled Brant with her eyes, secretly pleased that he even wanted to talk to her after she'd yelled at him this afternoon. The bed had come as such a shock, she knew she hadn't been gracious in the least. She should have thanked him, before telling him to send the crazy thing back to the store.

Of course, in her heart of hearts, it hadn't been what she had been hoping Brant would one day want to give her. She dreamed of a proper proposal, a heartfelt proposal, after waiting so long to hear one from him. Now, of course, the door was about to bang shut. She was about to have their baby—and everything else would have to be incidental.

"I will let you walk me home." Delight flooded her as Brant immediately stood.

"I should drive you."

"Walking's good for me." Her stomach muscles twisted around strangely, whether from the baby or Brant's presence, Grace couldn't be sure. "Maybe I will let you drive me."

"Are you okay?" His face was concerned as they left the Cafe. Brant waved absently to all the regulars as they got into his truck, but his mind was on Grace.

She hadn't answered him. She was so silent and pale that he was worried. Pulling into the driveway, he got out, walking around to help her down. "You look a bit peaked, or something. It's because I upset you, isn't it? I should have asked you, Grace. I should have—"

"I've got a little bit of an upset stomach." Grace interrupted, stopping on the sidewalk under the full, spreading limbs of an ancient oak tree. "I could be at the beginning of my labor."

"What?" Brant's face paled to match hers.

"Or I could not be," she said, turning to hurry toward her house.

"Wait just a cotton-pickin' minute here! How can you be at the beginning of labor?" He followed her breakneck pace easily.

"I'm not sure. It could be nothing."

"Grace, stop!" he roared. "Either it's labor, or it's nothing, but it can't be both. Which is it?"

"Most likely labor." She let them in the front door, running a hand over her forehead. "Whew! It's hot out there."

"You need to sit down. You need to rest. You need a glass of something cold to drink." Brant began pacing through the den after he situated her on the floral-printed divan in the den. "We need diapers. Have you gotten diapers?" At the shake of her head, he began pacing again, "We need formula. No. We're breast-feeding."

"The baby is breast-feeding," Grace reminded him wryly.

He stopped his pacing for only a split second to glance her way. Totally ignoring her attempt to tease him, he kept right on going. "Did we buy enough clothes for the baby when we were in New York?"

"I think a little pack of T-shirts in the beginning will do fine." She had to grin at Brant's lack of composure. "Brant, could you sit down for a moment? You're making me feel like I need to get up and clean out a bookcase or scrub shower walls with a toothbrush."

"You're not doing anything." He sank into a chair next to her. "Jeez. I don't think I can do anything. My brain's just gone on the blink."

She laughed, amazed by the sight of strong, stubborn Brant completely undone by the advent of a baby. "Maybe you should go home and rest."

"I'm not leaving." He looked out a window, then crossed to another window. "Listen, you make me a list, and I'll go get whatever's needed. I'll leave long enough to do that. But I'm spending the night with you, Grace, whether it's in the big bed, the guest room, or the sofa. You might need me."

Cramps hit in the middle of her belly, and Grace shifted a bit to ease them. "Maggie's coming over."

"Fine. The whole damn cafe can come over. But I'm staying."

"I think I'd like that." Grace smiled, a trifle uneasy from the sudden shifting of a baby inside her. "This baby has usually been so active, always doing flips in my belly. He's been so still today, it had me worried. But he's right back on track now."

"That's it! You're going to Doc Delancey's. No point in worrying if there's nothing to worry about."

"No!" She leaned back into the sofa, stretching a bit. "Now, listen, Brant. These are the ground rules. Only one of us is going through delivery, and that's me. So, your job is to be strong, to be a guide, and let me be the nervous one, okay? I've already talked to the doctor, and he thinks I'm fine. I was just voicing a bit of woman worry out loud, but you're not supposed to get all wound up.''

''You want reassurance.'' From his baby guide research, he remembered that was part of his job. And patience. He'd been very short of that.

''Yes, I do.''

''Reassurance.'' He adopted a gruff persona. ''Everything's gonna be fine, Grace. That little baby's just taking a breather before he comes squalling into the world.''

''That's better.'' She laughed. ''Ooh, I don't want to laugh.''

''What is it?'' He leapt to her side.

Grace took a deep breath. ''It's time I sent you to the store for baby stuff, I think.''

He looked at her carefully. ''I think I've changed my mind about leaving you. Let me go check what all they stuck up in the nursery, and then I'll make up a list of what's needed for John and Maggie to go pick up at the store. I know you'll do just fine, Grace, but I don't want to leave you.''

She sighed happily, feeling the gathering of new hope mixed with new life inside her. ''Oh, that sounds so nice, Brant.''

''What does?'' He wasn't paying attention as he rooted around for a pencil and paper.

''What you just said.'' Grace closed her eyes with contentment.

''I said I didn't want to leave…hey, lady,'' he said, putting the pencil and paper down immediately.

He crossed the room to sit on the sofa next to her, pulling her close. "Haven't I said that?"

"I don't think so." She met his dark blue eyes. "Maybe I've been so hurt that you left that I haven't heard you if you did say it."

"Maybe I should just add convincing to the list of patience and reassurance a pregnant woman needs. Grace, honey," he said, burying his face in her neck, "I goofed when I moved the bed in here, I'll admit. What I was trying to say was that I don't want to ever leave you again. I shouldn't have the first time. But I did, and doing it taught me one thing." He looked up to gaze into her eyes. "I couldn't ever forget you."

"Really?"

"Really." He put his hand over hers, which rested on her belly. "I'm just glad you had this little guy waiting around to knock some sense into my head. Being a father has forced me to reprioritize. You come first, babe."

"Oh, Brant." Sentimental tears jumped into her eyes. "That's so sweet."

"It's true. I want to take good care of you and the little man." He sat up straight. "Hey, what are you going to name him?"

"Brant."

"That's good for a start."

"Mmm. Brant Wyndford Barclay."

"I don't like that!"

"Wyndford *is* a bit stuffy," Grace agreed.

He cocked his eyebrow at her. "That's not what I mean!"

"I know." Grace gave him a gentle smile. "But

I can't do anything about the Barclay part right now.''

"Will you ever?"

She knew what he was asking. "Maybe. I think so. Right now, I'm so scared, I'm not sure. Can we have this discussion again when my stomach isn't upset?''

Brant jumped to his feet. "Can I get you something?''

"Some more of those wonderful words you were whispering in my ear a minute ago?''

He dropped next to her, wrapping his arms around her. "You should go upstairs and get changed into something extremely comfortable. I'll find an old movie on TV for us to watch, and root around in your refrigerator for some snacks. Then we'll just wait out the countdown.''

"Okay." She started to get up from the sofa, but he clasped her to him for one last hug. "Grace, I intend to tell you for the rest of my life how much I care about you. In the back of my mind, I can't forget that I'm a product of my environment. If I ever slip up and forget, will you give me a small reminder?''

"Like a frying pan upside the head?''

"I don't think it will ever take that much," he replied, his expression very serious. "There was never anyone for me but you, Grace. I took you for granted. That's all there is to it, the long and the short. I expected you to go along with my vision of our relationship. I didn't want to get married, but I didn't expect you to leave me. In my mind, it was always me and you, together, forever. When you asked about marriage, my only reaction was to run.

I've worked through what I was running from, but it wasn't you." He touched her hair, tenderly brushing it away from her face so he could see all of her features. "I wasn't running from you. I was running from me."

"Oh, Brant." She snuggled close for an enfolding hug.

"You have another commitment from me," he said huskily against her hair. "I'll teach my son how special his mother is. I will help him to see the difference between giving, and being afraid to give. I have to, you know." He put his head against hers. "I want my son to know that there's nothing to be afraid of when it comes to love."

BRANT JERKED AWAKE, glancing at his watch in the darkness. Four o'clock in the morning. He'd heard a moan, and it wasn't coming from the bed he was in.

"Grace!" he called, jumping from the bed. They'd fallen asleep in the California king size bed so that both of them could stretch out comfortably. "Where are you?"

"In here."

Her reply was more of a moan, and Brant hurried into the connecting washroom. "What is it?"

"Plain old labor pains," she told him.

"What are you doing in here? Why didn't you wake me up?"

She looked as pale as the white ceramic tiles in the bathroom. "I wanted you to get some rest. There's nothing you can do about labor pains, Brant. Go back to sleep." Her face pinched alarmingly.

"Come on in here," he told her. "Let me see if I can find you a position where you can relax."

She in no way looked relaxed to him. There were no socks or slippers on her feet, and her hair was tangled. He wondered if she was cold.

He drew her to him. "Maybe you'll be happier in the nursery in your old bed." At least it had the white lace canopy and sheets and all the trimmings. He hadn't had the chance to buy the accoutrements for this one. They'd merely pulled out a few blankets and pillows and made do. Obviously he'd slept great in the enormous, hardly made bed, while she'd been miserable.

"I'm doing fine." She moaned slightly, rubbing her stomach. "Maggie called after she closed the Cafe and suggested I rock." She bent her knees a little in a slight lunge and shifted back and forth on her feet. "Like that. It does seem to help. So, I've been rocking and walking."

"What can I do?"

She shook her head. "Just be here for me."

Fat lot of good he was doing her. He hadn't even heard the phone ring. "Come here," he said, helping her to the bed. Leaning against the wall where a headboard should have been, Brant pulled her up against him so that her back was facing him and he could support her stomach with his palms.

"That feels better," she sighed.

They sat like that for a while. Grace tried to doze in between contractions. After an hour, when another particularly agonizing spell hit her, he frowned at his watch in the dimness. The contractions seemed to be coming faster, maybe ten minutes apart. He wished greatly that he'd spent more time going over the baby manuals.

This baby seemed determined to be on the early introduction course.

"*Oh-h-h,*" Grace moaned.

"That's it. I'm calling Doc Delancey. Roll over here and lay on your side, babe." He helped Grace curl up, covered her with one of the mismatched blankets and headed for the phone. "Where's the number?" he muttered, finally resorting to calling information. Brant felt the taste of panic in his mouth. He didn't know the first thing about what he was supposed to be doing, and Grace wanted him to be patient, reassuring and convincing.

He'd read the page in the book that said women in the throes of delivery sometimes yelled at, perhaps even cursed, the man who'd gotten them into this predicament. He hoped Grace would go easy on him. It was probably best if he got her on to the hospital where she could have trained physicians and nurses helping her instead of him.

"Please page Dr. Delancey," he commanded the answering service who took his call.

"Is there an emergency?" the irritating woman asked.

"No. Yes! My wife's—my baby's having a baby. Wait. I'm having a baby. Jeez!" Brant exploded. "Will you just page the damn doctor!"

"Right away, sir," the clipped tones came back at him, "if you'll give me the phone number where the patient can be reached."

Brant gave her the number before slamming the phone back on the cradle. He cast a guilty glance at the ceiling. Hopefully he hadn't awakened Grace if she'd been managing two minutes of sleep. The phone shrilled, and he pounced on it.

"Hello?"

"This is Dr. Delancey."

At the calm voice, Brant told himself to slow down. Women had babies every day, and he could make it through his woman doing it. "Doctor, this is Brant Durning."

"Hello, Brant. How are you?"

He was fine except for the sweat soaking the underarms of his T-shirt. "I'm holding up. I think."

"Ah. How is Grace?"

"Better than me."

"It's normal for you to feel this way." Dr. Delancey laughed. "Do we have contractions?"

"Best as I can tell, they're about ten minutes apart and getting more intense. Although I was asleep for most of them."

"They weren't that bad if you slept through them. Grace is probably just now getting warmed up. This isn't false labor to have continued this long, so why don't you put her overnight bag in the car and come on down to the hospital?"

"Overnight bag?" Had Grace packed one?

"Well, really she'll need very little, and as the hospital is close, you—"

"I can handle an overnight bag, Dr. Delancey. Anything else?"

"No, just don't forget Grace. And you'll need a car seat eventually. The hospital won't let you go home without the baby in a proper car seat."

"Okay." His mind was so frantic he hoped he could remember.

"Now, don't rush to the hospital and have a wreck. She's still got some time to go. Proceed at a calm pace."

"Okay." Brant took a deep breath. "Thanks, Doctor. Proceed at a clam place."

Brig Delancey chuckled. "See you in a bit."

Brant vaulted the stairs. Grace was still rolled into a ball. "How are you doing?"

She tried to smile. "Same."

"Do you have an overnight bag packed?"

"It's in the closet."

Great. That was the hard part, because he sure wouldn't have known what to put in it. "Let's try to get you dressed."

"I don't think so. I'm going as is." Grace jumped from the bed and began a frantic rocking to and fro, breathing deeply until the pain passed. "I'll worry about being pretty some other time, but no one's going to see me at five o'clock in the morning."

He liked her practical attitude. "Now, is there anything else you want me to get you?" he asked, helping her to the stairwell.

"Call Maggie."

"Now?"

"Now." Grace slowly walked down the stairs. "She's my labor coach."

"Labor coach." Brant frowned but picked up the phone and called Maggie. After talking for a brief moment, he went outside, seeing Grace already huddled in his truck. Locking the door behind him, he hurried to the driver's side. "Rats! I forgot the overnight bag!"

"I got it." Grace's lips looked stiff with pain as she talked. "It's in the truck bed."

"Oh. Good thing you're handling this so well, because I'm sure not."

A bloodcurdling howl emitted from the woman he loved. He stared at her in astonishment.

"Great day! What's happening?"

Grace panted wildly as she arched against the seat. "I'm having a baby, what do you think? Get me to the hospital!"

Brant jammed the pedal to the floor, flying out of the driveway. Behind him he saw cruiser lights flare in the night. Slowing down, loud honking sounded as the car swept around him. Maggie's arm fluttered outside the passenger window.

"Your police escort just arrived, babe. I'll have you at the hospital in no time."

Following John at a decent speed, Brant let his mind go on autopilot. He didn't worry about what entrance to the hospital to go to. He didn't worry about how he was going to get her from the truck to the safe, helping hands of trained personnel. He just put Grace's head in his lap. "Squeeze my arm if you get another pain. And I'm ready for another shriek if you need to. In fact, don't be surprised if I yell along with you."

"Shut up, Brant."

"Okay, babe." Trailing behind the cruiser, he pulled up outside the emergency entrance. In an instant, Maggie was at Grace's door, opening it and carefully helping her out.

"John'll park your truck," she called to Brant. "Let's get her inside."

"You guys act like I'm dying. I'm just having a baby." Grace gritted between teeth she couldn't unlock for the pain.

"You let us engage in hysteria, you focus on the baby," Maggie instructed her.

"If I'd said that to her, it wouldn't have made her feel better." Brant shot Maggie a glance over Grace's bowed head. "I'm glad you're here."

"You're the man that got her into this, honey. Me, I had nothing to do with it." Maggie laughed heartily. "Come on, Grace, step up here and we'll have you inside in a jiff."

"Oh, Maggie!" Grace's voice sounded torn. "There's an alien inside my body."

"I know," the other woman said soothingly. "And he's trying to land his spaceship. Breathe. Breathe."

Brant hurried to the desk to announce Grace's presence. A nurse with a face that looked as if it had seen one too many birthing mothers said, "Are you the labor coach?"

"No. She is." He pointed to Maggie.

"Only immediate family and her labor coach are allowed in the labor room with the patient."

The nurse began leading Grace away. "Maggie!" he shouted. "I just pulled rank on you. I'm the man who got her here, I go in the labor room. You sit in the waiting room with John."

Maggie grinned. "Whatever you say. Call me if you need a break."

"I thought she was the labor coach," the old nurse mentioned.

Brant shook his head. "It was a misunderstanding. I'm doing the coaching around here."

"Are you sure, Brant?" Grace looked wan. "I didn't think you'd want to—"

"I want to. Now shh-shh." He allowed the battleaxe nurse to take her to a table. "Relax if you can. Squeeze my hand if it helps."

"I'm going to check you now," the nurse said.

Brant closed his eyes, feeling squeamish. The woman didn't look near as gentle as he'd want her to be, but Grace never batted an eyelash.

"She's at eight," the nurse announced. "We're going to have to get down to business fast."

Brant stayed out of the way while Grace was prepped. Dr. Brig Delancey strode in, taking command. "Good job, Grace," he said.

"I don't feel like I'm doing a good job. I want to quit now," she moaned.

"Hang in there. The epidural will start working fast." He gave Brant a shrewd eyeing as the anaesthetist arrived. "You going to be all right, Brant?"

"I'm fine," Brant replied indignantly. He couldn't pay too much attention to the doctor as he was closely watching the anaesthetist approach Grace's back. "For crying out loud, I've seen plenty of cows calve. I think I can handle—"

He lost his voice when the anaesthetist pierced a wicked looking needle into the area around Grace's spine.

"Whoa! Dad going down!" Dr. Delancey called.

Grace watched them gather around the man who had fathered her child. The nurse with the stern face continued to hold Grace's hand, patting it.

"You know he'll get paid back for that comment in his next life," she told the nurse. "He'll come back as a woman."

Together they watched Brant being helped to his feet.

"Oh, God, no," he moaned, overhearing Grace's prediction. "Anything but that."

Dr. Delancey propped him into a chair. "Stay there until you catch your breath."

He already felt immensely better now that they'd finished with Grace's back. She was lying down, already looking a lot more comfortable. "There's your baby," she said, pointing to the monitor.

Waves moved across the monitor. Amazement filled Brant at what he could see. An instant connection to his child jolted him.

He couldn't wait to hold the tiny person who was going to change their lives. New emotion for Grace, something he'd always felt, magnified a hundred percent at the sight of those waves. Unable to speak, he hurried off to get Grace a cup of ice chips. "I know what I'm supposed to be doing," he told her, kissing her on the forehead when he returned. "Hope I didn't worry you when I hit the ground."

"No." Her voice was calm. "We're in a hospital if you concuss yourself."

He chuckled, then sat in a chair nearby to hold her hand and wait for the arrival.

IT COULDN'T HAVE BEEN more than an hour later that Grace was wheeled to the delivery room. Brant had gone out once to give John and Maggie an update, but now as he tagged along behind Grace's gurney, he felt a peculiar churning in his stomach. The big moment was at hand.

"You wait outside a minute, Brant," Dr. Delancey told him. "We'll get you shortly."

Immediately the operating room doors closed in his face. "What the—"

Glancing to each end of the hall, he saw no one

to tell him what was going on inside the OR that he couldn't participate in. "Why, why—"

In the operating room, the nurse rolled her eyes as she glanced at Dr. Delancey. "I figure you've got about thirty seconds to give her that last injection before Mr. Durning—"

"I'm sorry," Brant huffed, coming to stand alongside Grace, "I can't wait outside, Dr. Delancey. You'll have to call security—"

"It's all right, Brant." The doctor grinned. "We're all finished. Let's get to delivering a baby."

Sweat popped out on Brant's forehead. He desperately chanted his mantra of ice chips and patience. Grace pushed, and he supported her back.

Suddenly baby cries filled the room.

"Oh! Oh!" Grace cried, her face alight with joy.

"Oh, my Lord." Brant's tone was thunderstruck as he stared at the infant. "I can't believe I just saw that."

He reached out to touch the baby, but it was whisked away before he got a good look. Nurses quickly measured, wiped clean and weighed the squalling infant. Planting a tearful kiss on Grace, Brant kept a watchful eye on what they were doing with his child. "I can't believe it, I can't believe it," he repeated. "You're so brave. You did such a good job. You're amazing."

Grace's eyes sparkled under his praise.

"Everything's all there, all fingers and toes," the doctor announced. "Perfect health."

"Here you go, Dad," the wizened nurse said, handing the wailing baby to Brant, "isn't she beautiful?"

"She!" Grace and Brant glanced at each other, astonished.

"It's a girl?" Brant asked, astonished.

"Yep. Guess it was her thumb they saw on the sonogram." Brig Delancey grinned hugely, but Grace and Brant never saw it, never heard his quip. Brant took the baby from the nurse, holding her in his hands as if she were most fragile crystal. As if he were holding a miracle he'd waited for all his life.

He was transfixed by her rosy mouth, by her waving little fists.

"Grace Barclay," he said quietly but firmly, "if you don't agree to marry me right this instant, I'm going to cry right here in front of my little girl."

Their eyes met over the squirming bundle. Grace was exhausted, but she smiled at him. "That baby appeals to you, does she?" she asked, falling even more deeply in love at the marveling expression on Brant's face.

"This baby's a tractor rider if I ever saw one." He glanced down quickly, but not before Grace saw the tears in his eyes. "She's strong." He let one of the minuscule fingers wrap around his.

Grace's doubts suddenly washed away. "I'll marry you, Brant," she said softly, but with conviction. It was the only thing she could say. She loved the man far too much to hold out any longer.

The nurse took the baby from Brant. He bent over to press a lingering kiss against Grace's lips. "I love you."

Though Grace had dreamed of hearing Brant say just those words, it still startled her into her own admission. "I love you, too."

"I'm not saying this just because of the baby," he

said huskily, "though watching you give birth was the most incredible, beautiful, frightening thing I have ever seen." He took a deep breath. "I have always loved you, Grace. I always will."

He enfolded her into as much of a hug as he could manage with nurses cleaning her up. The nurses and doctor were acting as if they weren't listening, but several smiles lit the operating room.

Happy tears seeped from Grace's eyes. "This is the happiest day of my life."

"It's the happiest day of mine. It's a good thing you didn't get over me."

"How could I? You wouldn't let me."

"I couldn't." Brant closed his eyes for just a moment. "I never told you this before, but you are the only woman I have ever loved."

"I knew that. I knew it all along."

"How?" Brant met Grace's warm gaze.

"Cami told me."

"Cami! I'm going to have a talk with that sister of mine."

"Oh? And what are you going to say to her?"

Nearby, their little daughter was raising a ruckus, and Brant smiled tolerantly. He touched his lips to Grace's. "I'm going to tell her that she can't keep a secret...and then I'm going to kiss her for sending me to the Wedding Wonderland for her dress."

Another wail went up from the baby, who appeared to dislike being charted or weighed or graphed. Grace shot Brant a teasing grin. "She'll want you to buy her a wedding dress one day."

"I know." He chuckled. "But since her mother owns the shop, I can look forward to that day."

Epilogue

Three weeks after the birth of Margaret Elise, a wedding party was in full swing at the Double D ranch.

"I'd like to toast the lady who's putting the double back in the D around here," Brant said loudly to the assembled guests, lifting a champagne glass. "Grace, you've made me the happiest man alive. It isn't often a man gets two women for the price of one."

Hoots of laughter followed his comment. Grace raised her glass in a silent toast to her new husband. For a man who had been marriage-shy, he seemed to be taking to it with gusto. He made a tall, handsome groom, dressed in a formal evening tux as black as his hair. She admired the way he looked, knowing that this man who made her heart thunder was happy to be hers.

Tearing her gaze away, Grace glanced around the lawn. Maggie, as usual, had outdone herself on the catering and decorating and everything else. Sheriff John had given Grace away, whispering to her as he stood beside her at the altar that Brant hadn't taken his eyes off of her since the moment she began her walk down the aisle. Brant's eyes had indeed been on her, protectively, possessively, and Grace had known complete joy in finally wearing one of the dream-come-true gowns from the Wedding Wonderland.

"Isn't she adorable?"

Grace glanced toward Brant's parents. Though her own parents were traveling on another continent and hadn't been able to rearrange their tickets fast enough to get home for the wedding, Elsa had certainly kept her word. Right now, she and Michael Durning were staring down at baby Margaret. Already way too spoiled, and dressed in the lovely gown Grace had admired in New York. Brant had called her friend, Jana, a few days after Margaret was born to have the gown sent to Texas as a surprise for Grace. He teasingly referred to it as the baby bridal gown, which never failed to make Grace laugh. She was delighted, and even a little humbled by his instant, awestruck attachment to his little girl.

Behind Elsa and Michael, Dr. Nelson stood a discreet distance away, happy, it seemed, to be wherever Elsa was. Texas agreed with him. While Elsa helped Grace give a bridesmaids' luncheon today, he'd roamed off to Waxahachie to see the infamous courthouse where, long ago, a sculptor had carved fascinating feelings about a woman into the stone.

Michael Durning would always be odd-man-out, but he appeared to lavish attention on Margaret— maybe the way he hadn't on Brant and Cami.

Grace's glance flicked to Brant's sister. Cami was a lovely matron of honor, and now beginning to show. Grace grinned at her new sister-in-law. There was a lot the two of them would get to share....

Happy-go-lucky Tilly had been the recipient of Dr. Delancey's conversation for the last half hour, Grace noticed. Kyle Macaffee had come, too, a bit bashful and very brave, she thought gratefully, since he might have preferred staying away. She would certainly have understood. Her sister, Hope, serving as her other wedding attendant, had asked the handsome veterinarian for assistance with something, and the two had been engaged in conversation ever since. Somehow, Kyle didn't look bashful anymore. Since Hope was staying in Grace's house for the summer so the baby could be close by the shop, who knew?

"Time to throw the bouquet, Grace!" Cami helped her up the stairwell far enough to toss the flowers backward. "All you single women line up for a chance!"

Some women moved forward readily, others balked but were shoved close by friends. Grace closed her eyes and tossed.

"Tilly!" Cami exclaimed as the waitress caught the flying bouquet of whites roses and satin ribbons. "You're next!"

The whole room erupted in laughter as Brant needed no urging to come take the garter from Grace's leg. He did a bit of a rooster dance as he got closer, strutting while the men got into place.

"Stop, Brant!" Grace laughed, somewhat embarrassed by her new husband's antics.

Ignoring her, he refused to give the crowd much of a glimpse of her leg, instead snaking his hand up to find the garter, all the while wiggling his eyebrows at the onlookers. Suddenly he snatched it off and fired it from the tip of his finger.

The little piece of blue and white satin flew across the room—and hit Sheriff John squarely in the face even though he tried to duck.

"Sheriff John!" Brant called. "The next man to find himself at the altar."

"Not me!" he called good-naturedly, though Grace noticed he glanced Maggie's way. She shook her head at the sheriff. Grace hoped that wouldn't be the case forever.

Brant leaned over, kissing her and stealing all thoughts of her guests from her mind. "Mrs. Brant Durning, Mrs. Grace Barclay Durning, other half of the Double D, your overlarge bed awaits you upstairs. It has been properly short-sheeted by some pranksters, because I heard them complaining greatly about the difficulties in trying to short-sheet a California king-size bed. Shall we inspect their handiwork?"

Grace laughed, getting to her feet. Out of the corner of her eye, she saw Buzz and Purvis doing an excellent job of passing out birdseed. "Did you arrange for the limo driver to drive us around long enough for our guests to leave?" she asked. "When I get you back home, I want you all to myself."

"Not near as much as I want you all to myself," Brant told her, tucking her close as they prepared to run through the shower of falling birdseed. "The chase is over, Mrs. Durning, but the best part has just begun."

THE NEXT DAY was considerably quieter around the Yellowjacket Cafe. In the kitchen, Maggie gave Sheriff John's hand a solid whack with her wooden spatula. Buzz could hear the resounding crack at his checkerboard, but he barely noticed it. He had something far greater on his mind.

"Playing checkers isn't as much fun as it used to be," he told Purvis Brown.

"I know." Purvis looked around the cafe. He didn't have to ask his friend what he meant. With Grace and Brant honeymooning, and Cami and Dan busy combining ranches, it was going to be too slow for at least a little while. "Still, it's better than this crazy contraption of my grandkid's." He pulled a Nintendo computer game from his pocket.

"Gimme that!" Buzz said, impatient to see what the buttons could do. After a moment, he sorrowfully shook his head, giving it back to Purvis. "This generation's gonna grow up without knowing the benefits of a thinking man's game like checkers."

"Yep," Purvis agreed. "Strategizing. That's what makes men succeed on the battlefield, the football field, and everywhere else." Purvis put the game away, glancing at his friend shrewdly. "So, who can we work on now?"

Buzz sidled his gaze across to the kitchen where Tilly was picking up short orders. "There's Maggie and Sheriff John."

"That'd be like sifting sand through the eye of a needle," Purvis commented. "Impossible." He thought for a moment. "What about the new doc? Dr. Delancey? Last I checked, he ain't got nobody."

"Maybe." Buzz rubbed his chin. "Tilly ain't, either."

Purvis pulled his gaze away from the kitchen and the long-legged waitress. He shook his head. "Naw. Ain't nobody been able to stay with her long enough to hear the bell."

It was a many-told rumor about the waitress. Men

said that trying to date Tilly Channing was like trying to stay on a bronc for eight seconds.

Buzz rubbed his palms together, his eyes lit with sudden excitement. ''Then again, finding Tilly a man just might be fun. And there's our good-hearted veterinarian, Dr. Kyle Macaffee, who's still on the loose....''

Purvis nodded his satisfied agreement. ''Your move, old friend.''

*Their idea of a long night is a sexy
woman and a warm bed—
not a squalling infant!
To them, a "bottle" means champagne—
not formula!
But these men are about to get
a wake-up call...
They're about to become*

ACCIDENTAL DADS

Join us in November 1998 for

#751 SHE'S HAVING HIS BABY
by Linda Randall Wisdom

Available at your favorite retail outlet.

HARLEQUIN®
Makes any time special ™

Look us up on-line at: http://www.romance.net   HARDAD2

Looking For More Romance?

Visit Romance.net

Look us up on-line at: http://www.romance.net

Check in daily for these and other exciting features:

Hot off the press

View all current titles, and purchase them on-line.

What do the stars have in store for you?

Horoscope

Hot deals

Exclusive offers available only at Romance.net

Plus, don't miss our interactive quizzes, contests and bonus gifts.

PWEB

Can tossing a coin in the Trevi Fountain really make wishes come true? Three average American women are about to find out when they throw...

3 COINS IN A FOUNTAIN

For Gina, Libby and Jessie, the trip to Rome wasn't what they'd expected. They went seeking romance and ended up finding disaster! What harm could throwing a coin bring?

IF WISHES WERE HUSBANDS...
Debbi Rawlins—September

IF WISHES WERE WEDDINGS...
Karen Toller Whittenburg—October

IF WISHES WERE DADDIES...
Jo Leigh—November

3 COINS IN A FOUNTAIN
If wishes could come true...

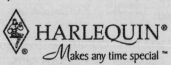

HARLEQUIN®
Makes any time special ™

Available at your favorite retail outlet.

Look us up on-line at: http://www.romance.net   HAR3C

the holiday heart

You loved the Holiday men so much, we're bringing you more!

Meet Richard Holiday. He's great looking, he's successful, he's urbane—but when he becomes guardian of his niece and nephews, he's out of his league! Richard can't tell a turkey from a chicken, let alone plan a Thanksgiving dinner for his new family. What's he to do?

Find out in Harlequin American Romance

#752 DOORSTEP DADDY
by Linda Cajio
November 1998

Everyone loves the *Holidays*....

Available at your favorite retail outlet.

HARLEQUIN®
Makes any time special ™

Look us up on-line at: http://www.romance.net

HARDD

**SEXY, POWERFUL MEN NEED
EXTRAORDINARY WOMEN WHEN THEY'RE**

Destined for Love

Take a walk on the wild side this October
when three bestselling authors weave wondrous stories
about heroines who use their extraspecial abilities to
achieve the magic and wonder of love!

HATFIELD AND McCOY
by HEATHER GRAHAM POZZESSERE

LIGHTNING STRIKES
by KATHLEEN KORBEL

MYSTERY LOVER
by ANNETTE BROADRICK

Available October 1998
wherever Harlequin and Silhouette books are sold.

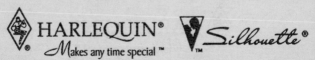

HARLEQUIN®
Makes any time special™

Silhouette®

Look us up on-line at: http://www.romance.net

PSBR1098

Mysterious, sexy, sizzling...

THE AUSTRALIANS

Stories of romance Australian-style, guaranteed to fulfill that sense of adventure!

This November look for

Borrowed—One Bride
by **Trisha David**

Beth Lister is surprised when Kell Hallam kidnaps her on her wedding day and takes her to his dusty ranch, Coolburna. Just who is Kell, and what is his mysterious plan? But Beth is even more surprised when passion begins to rise between her and her captor!

The Wonder from Down Under: where spirited women win the hearts of Australia's most independent men!

Available November 1998
where books are sold.

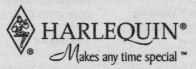

HARLEQUIN®
Makes any time special ™

Look us up on-line at: http://www.romance.net   PHAUS5

COMING NEXT MONTH

#749 IF WISHES WERE...DADDIES by Jo Leigh
Three Coins in a Fountain
Jessica Needham wished to be left alone, particularly by Nick Carlucci—
but she was having his baby. She'd convinced herself he'd never need to
know—right up until she opened her door to find Nick on the other
side....

#750 SIGN ME, SPEECHLESS IN SEATTLE by Emily Dalton
As the title star of the popular column "Ask Aunt Tilly," Mathilda McKinney
dispensed advice to the lovelorn and the troubled. But who would advise
Mathilda, now that drop-dead-gorgeous duke Julian Rothwell was steamed
at her counsel—and demanded Tilly herself as payment!

#751 SHE'S HAVING HIS BABY by Linda Randall Wisdom
Accidental Dads
Caitlin O'Hara and Jake Roberts. They went together like peanut butter
and jelly. Friends since the first day of kindergarten, they shared everything,
including Friday-night pizza and war stories from the romance trenches.
But there were some things you didn't even ask your best friend—like "Can
you make me pregnant?" Or did you?

#752 DOORSTEP DADDY by Linda Cajio
The Holiday Heart
Richard Holiday: Single, sexy—and up to his ears in dirty diapers and
raging hormones, toddlers, teenagers and kids in between! But was he ready
to give up his bachelorhood? The three happy children made his house feel
like a real home.... The only thing missing was a wife....

AVAILABLE THIS MONTH:

**#745 IF WISHES WERE...
WEDDINGS**
Karen Toller Whittenburg

#746 DADDY BY DESTINY
Muriel Jensen

#747 MAKE ROOM FOR BABY
Cathy Gillen Thacker

**#748 COWBOY COOTCHIE-
COO**
Tina Leonard

Look us up on-line at: http://www.romance.net